SUMMERS OF THE WILD ROSE

about the author

Rosemary Harris is a Londoner, but spent her early years moving from place to place, 'being slightly educated by different schools. My first stories were dictated when I was about four or five – the central figure was a greyhound, called, oddly enough, Greyhound. He had endless adventures underground by the light of one naked light bulb suspended from a tunnel roof.'

Her first books were for adults and included two thrillers; then in 1968 she published her first children's book, *The Moon in the Cloud,* which was awarded the Library Association's Carnegie Medal. Two sequels followed: *The Shadow on the Sun* and *The Bright and Morning Star*. Since then she has written adult thrillers and picture book stories, but she is perhaps best known for her teenage novels. These include the fascinating science-fiction sequence *A Quest for Orion* and *Tower of the Stars,* and *Zed,* a powerful story of hostage-taking told from the point of view of the child who is caught up in the drama.

SUMMERS OF THE WILD ROSE

Rosemary Harris

LONDON · BOSTON

First published in Great Britain in 1987
by Faber and Faber Limited
3 Queen Square London WC1N 3AU
This paperback edition first published in 1991

Printed in England by Clays Ltd, St Ives plc

A CIP record for this book
is available from the British Library.

ISBN: 0-571-16323-8

Heidenröslein
(The Little Heath Rose)

Once a young lad saw a briar
Wild rose in the heather.
She was fresh and morning-fair;
Joyfully he hurried near,
Briar sweet to gather –

Wild rose, wild rose, wild rose red,
Wild rose in the heather.

He declared, I'm plucking thee,
Wild rose of the heather.
Wild rose warned, I'm pricking thee.
Thou shalt then remember me
And shalt pluck me never.

Wild rose, wild rose, wild rose red,
Wild rose in the heather.

Heedless lad, he went to take
Wild rose from the heather.
Wild rose used her thorns to rake –
No resistance she might make
Could defend her ever.

Wild rose, wild rose, wild rose red,
Wild rose in the heather.

GOETHE
(translated by RH)

1965

1

Clare scowled at me quite ferociously across the table, pushed back her floppy chestnut hair, and said, 'Now, why are you ganging up against me with my mother, Nell? None of it's your business, is it?'

I could have hit her. She had turned up unexpectedly at my office, on a day when I should have been lunching with a rising young pianist, discussing his future and trying to explain that his views on concert fees were unreal. I could only hope that he wouldn't walk into this restaurant now and find me reluctantly entertaining my usually-favourite niece instead. Or was 'entertaining' the right word? Clare had eaten little, and in ominous silence, until we reached the pudding stage.

Restraining the impulse to slap, I said, 'Do drink some of this delicious wine, and tell me exactly why you think I'm ganging up with Laura.'

'She did write to you, didn't she? I was at home last weekend, and I found the letter in her bag.'

'I see. And did you steam open the envelope?'

'Nell!'

'Why jump to conclusions that I'm ganging up? I don't have to agree with everything your mother says, do I? But it's true she wrote to me.'

The letter, scrawled in my younger sister's almost indecipherable hand, had reached me the day before.

Riverside Cottage,
Thamesbank

12th June, 1965

Eleanor, my dear,

Just a tiny line about Clare, darling. I'm worried, and you know what her father is, just sits there complaining. Of course she needs fun, we're the least possessive of parents, but now we feel her music's leading her into *undesirable situations*. I don't mean that they – *he* takes drugs, at least I hope not, but they – he's different from us. No good blinking facts, is it? If nature meant us to mingle we'd see swallows mating with goldfinches, which they *never do*.

(Laura being delicately racist, without wishing to say so outright.)

Clare has been offered a place with that famous Youth Orchestra which has a Summer School in France before going on tour. She's determined to go, gets *most* unpleasant if I point out *certain objections*. Bringing up children is impossible, these days – though you wouldn't know about that.

You've always been marvellous with Clare, and she's really fond of you. Do talk to her for us, persuade her this project's all wrong, tell her the orchestra's *lousy*, in spite of its reputation. She'd believe you – after all, you do run your own Agency, clever you. Don't fail us, will you?

Much love,
Laura

P.S. Couldn't you speak to her of your own *bitter* past experience, which would be more meaningful than anything *I* could say? Oh dear, I'm afraid that's tactless, but you know I believe in being *frank*.

Remembering that letter, I also found myself remembering other moments in their past conflicts. Seven-year-old Clare saying sadly, 'Mummy won't let me have a puppy because they do piddle so, and she wants new carpet in the hall. *You* ask her to let me have a puppy, Nell.' Then Clare at fifteen, wailing, 'Mum won't let me go to stay with Mike, his family's mad on water sports, and she says it's unsafe. Nell, she makes me look such a fool, do *please* talk to her.' Now: 'Well, if you're not ganging up, can I read her letter?' asked Clare. 'Or would you tell me what she said?'

'Oh, Clare! If I broke your mother's confidence, how much would you trust me with yours, always supposing that you wanted to?'

She considered that. 'She does want you to try and stop me going to that Summer School, though. Doesn't she? I'm going, that's all – not even Laura's going to prevent me.'

'But I think it's a chance in a million for you,' I said. 'Congratulations on winning a place – it's wonderful luck, most young 'cellists like you would give their eyes for it. Not luck, either: you deserve it.'

Her sigh was relieved. 'I'm sorry, Nell. I didn't mean to be foul, only it's been dreadful with Laura, about – ' She gave me a swift sideways glance, and changed what she was going to say to, 'Would you write to Laura and tell her I must go?'

'But I've done that already. I told her that it was one of the few small doorways to the larger scene, and that all the greatest names in music give Master Classes there.'

'Oh Nell, thank you. She'd like that.'

'And I told her you'd be working like crazy from dawn to dusk, which wouldn't leave much time for – anything else.'

There was silence. Then Clare actually gave a delighted laugh. 'That was sweet of you, Nell. I suppose that means she told you too about – ' A look of appeal.

'Laura's always a bit incoherent, but there was something about goldfinches not mating with swallows, from which I deduced a boyfriend of a different race.'

'What a cliché, and how like Laura.'

'And that he'd been accepted for the orchestra too. But I do agree with you that it's not my business – unless you want it to be?'

She looked doubtful. 'I don't really want to keep talking about it just yet, not to anyone. 'Fact, I must rush now, he's waiting for me.' She began collecting her things together. 'I'd have brought him along, only I thought Laura had been getting at you first. It would be really nice, though, if you could meet some time. You do know that I just wanted to make sure that you hadn't – that you wouldn't – '

'Interfere?' I shook my head. 'I'll look forward to meeting him, whoever he is. But before you go, Clare, there's something you should know – you'll be seeing me around in the background at the Summer School, socializing and talent spotting. Maestro Strogani himself invited me weeks ago.'

Perhaps, beneath the fierce independence, she was wondering how she'd cope on her own, for I thought she almost looked relieved. She gave me a quick hug. 'I – we'll see you there, then.' She looked at me rather shyly. 'You know, Nell, it's funny, but when we were arguing Laura kept being mysterious and saying things like, "If Nell could talk to you about *her* experience." I bet that's partly why she wrote to you in the first place! But whatever was – '

'You mother thinks in terms of parallel lines,' I said lightly, 'but people's problems are seldom very alike, and anyway she's forgetting the generation gap.' I hesitated, before adding with some reluctance, 'If you do want to hear about it any time – well, perhaps it can help to know one's not the only person who ever floundered into quicksands. Hurry along now, honey, mustn't keep him waiting, specially if your mother's told him he's not a goldfinch. See you soon, with or without the boy-friend.'

'See you, Nell,' she said almost eagerly. 'Thanks for understanding. Thanks too for lunch. I'm sorry I bitched you.'

I watched her walk away: head up, steps light, music case swinging from her hand. I sighed. Perhaps it was just as well that Maestro Strogani had invited me to France, after all. At least I could lend a sympathetic ear to Clare's troubles if she felt herself more vulnerable in that combative world. Though need I have made that rash offer to discuss my own early youth with her? Even Laura had thought twice before doing so without my permission, she didn't like making me angry – or perhaps it was because she'd known less about my time in Austria than she pretended. I had never discussed it with her, nor had my parents, I felt sure. Probably she'd gleaned most of it by listening at doors after my return to England.

Anyway, those events of 1937 were not so long ago that recalling them couldn't bring back the bittersweet memories, the anguish; the happiness too like the crystallized sweetness remaining in an old-fashioned scentbottle. . . . Now I was in danger of turning sentimental. Surely young uncertain Nell Dobell was buried deep enough inside poised and successful Mrs. Hathaway not to make herself felt in unwelcome resurrection – surely by this time I could try to see her as dispassionately as someone whose story was once told me by someone else.

1937

2

It was the summer I was almost seventeen, backward enough by today's standards, all the same eager to try my wings away from home. School gave me my first real opportunity: our local grammar school, with its high musical reputation due to the strenuous efforts of Thomasina Armstrong, our music teacher – known to us as Tommy – and her nervous assistant Rudolph Scroggworthy, Ruddigore as we called him behind his back.

I was both a member of the school choir and a budding soloist. It was a challenging time for us all, since Tommy aimed high and had persuaded our Headmistress to let us enter a famous Young Singers and Instrumentalists Contest, with the later heats held at Innsbruck, where a distinguished panel of Adjudicators would decide our merits. The earlier stages had been exciting, urged on as we were by Tommy's vigorous, often scathing coaching, and the tremulous backing-up of Ruddigore. Half-way through the summer term we finally emerged victorious over a fine Welsh choir in Cardiff, and I came through unscathed in my own category of soloists.

Back at school Tommy sent for me to decide my Innsbruck programme.

'Work hard enough at your exercises, Eleanor, and you may not disgrace us. Think less of yourself and more about the school.'

'Oh yes, Miss Armstrong.'

'There's still quite a large British entry for the elimination round at Innsbruck, before the quarter-finals. Traditionally, one of your songs should be in the language of the host country; I'm satisfied that you're well enough grounded in German.'

I said tentatively, 'Couldn't I sing *"Liebst du um Schönheit"*?' I was crazy about Mahler that summer, having lately discovered his Rückert songs. Tommy, I was sure, would favour Schubert's *'Heidenröslein'*, which I had sung in Wales.

'Should you reach the semi-finals you may add a third song. We must consider your programme carefully.'

'Oh yes, Miss Armstrong.'

'Bring me your ideas next Saturday; if I can sacrifice my free time, so can you. Ten o'clock in the music school. That's all, child. Don't forget your exercises.'

I was leaving the room when she called after me, 'Eleanor! Your parents are making no objections?'

'They haven't said so.'

'Good. One or two parents are reconsidering, the situation in Austria being politically unsettled. Personally, I feel music overrides all differences, crosses all frontiers, and is invariably an influence for good. Don't forget that your father or mother must sign the form permitting you to go.'

I bicycled home through the Hampshire lanes. It was a glorious end of June day, and I felt peaceful and happy yet at the same time like a coil of energy, strung with expectation. The air was fresh though hazily golden. It had been that sort of summer altogether, with only the lightest of showers to help ripen young wheat and bring out the flower scents after rain. Dog-roses ran riot over hedgerows and copses, so that wherever I looked there were clusters of pink and white.

Everything seemed so calm and eternal that I could barely imagine trouble in some other country. Of course the papers were full of dark hints, and people often worried about Hitler and Mussolini, specially those who, like my father, had fought in the World War; but somehow it seemed impossible that we were being drawn towards the brink again. Particularly not on a day like this, of sun and birdsong, with meadowsweet massed in pale green and yellow fluffy clouds on banks and meadows.

'Your father and I have been considering the Austrian side, we never really thought you'd get so far,' my mother said that evening. 'And anyway it would mean your missing the end of summer term. And you may have no special exams coming up, but is it worth it, just for music?'

'Oh, Mother! Just? It's desperately important to me.'

My father was lighting his pipe. When it was drawing well he spoke in his deliberate lawyer's tones: 'I'm not too happy about your going to Austria, Nell. It hasn't been a stable place since their last Chancellor was assassinated. This fellow Schusnigg, their present one, won't be able to hold off Hitler's claims much longer. He's got some Nazi trouble-makers of his own.'

I knew the papers were full of rumours that Hitler was planning the annexation of Austria – the *Anschluss*.

'Oh, Dad. Please!'

'Oh, Nell,' he mimicked me, though kindly. '*Coups d'état* are no respecters of persons.'

'But surely something like that would – would take place in Vienna? We're not going near there. Even the really grand Adjudicators are coming to Innsbruck for the Final. It would be crashing bad luck if anything went wrong just then.'

'Yes, it would, old lady, yet crashing bad luck does happen.'

'But Germans and Austrians revere musicians, they truly do,' I argued. (Perhaps the wrong tack: there were nasty tales of what had happened to some of Germany's foremost Jewish musicians.) 'We're not going to Germany,' I added hastily.

'Sensibly not. There would be martial and uglier echoes underlying any national festival. Won't have my daughter singing the Horst Wessel song and Heil Hitling.'

'As if I would.'

'Put your foot down, Henry,' said my mother. 'The whole idea is ridiculous. What do you hope to gain from it, Nell?'

Oh, give me patience. 'It's just the most wonderful chance for me, that's all.' I handed my father a printed leaflet. 'Look at the Adjudicators who are coming for the soloists' final: Lotte Lehmann, Richard Strauss himself – '

My father's 'Mmmmm' on an upward note was more encouraging. 'And who's this person called von – von Karajan?'

'Oh, him – he's for the instrumentalists. Someone they've dug up from Aachen, somebody new,' I said. 'Mummie, my voice does come from your side of the family, doesn't it? You ought to understand,' I wheedled. 'After all, though you didn't train, you could have done.'

She gave me a frosty smile. 'Well, I wash my hands of it. Thank God Laura won't reach this independent stage just yet. If you go, it's your father's decision.'

'We'll think it over,' he said, puffing at his pipe.

'Daddy, the form needs signing now. If Tommy thinks I'm not coming she won't bother to coach me.'

My father took out his fountain pen and signed the form with a flourishing 'Henry Dobell'. 'There you are, Nell, for the present. But if things look like getting worse you must cancel.'

'Thanks, Dad.' I gave a huge sigh of relief. His kindness always made me vulnerable, nearly ready to give in on the spot. Nearly. Not quite.

On Saturday I waited for Tommy by the music school, regretting a morning spent indoors when a warm breeze was bringing lush summer scents from the downs. Tommy arrived briskly by bicycle, catching her skirt on the chain as she dismounted and swearing in an outspoken way. As I trailed after her into the school I found myself wondering what the Austrians would make of her eccentricity. Typically dotty Englishwoman?

'Here's the signed form, Miss Armstrong.'

'No objections, then?'

I shook my head, not meeting that gimlet gaze.

'Sit down, Eleanor, and let me hear your suggestions about what you should sing and your reasons for your choice.' We were expected to understand the whys and wherefores before we embarked on any song. Mumblings about feelings would fetch some blistering retort.

'I've tried matching up some songs that I know really well already. It was rather hard.'

'To put two or three songs together shouldn't tax your intelligence. Never make excuses for yourself, child. You're lucky to be starting with some knowledge of German, girls who have none will find it harder.'

Our language classes were first-rate anyway, and I had been helped by holidays abroad, my father always insisting we should get away whenever possible, however cheaply, to sun or snow or plain enjoyment. Often, we'd camped. 'Nell has every chance to be fluent in other tongues, and she can just about ask her way around,' he would complain. It wasn't truly so bad as that, but if I hoped for a career in music I should have to take more trouble –

'Eleanor, are you listening? I said that a largely Teutonic audience may sniff at putting a Somervell song alongside Schubert.'

'But as I'm English shouldn't I start with an English song?'

'Possibly. Though not, the first time they hear you, with one they certainly won't know.'

Slash, went her pencil.

'We want them concentrating more on you than on the song. At least, I suppose so?'

The pencil moved on down my poor little list, to the accompaniment of damping remarks: 'That song's too high for you and doesn't transpose well . . . that one's too difficult, even if you pull it off they won't believe their ears . . . "Where Corals Lie"?' A delicately-raised eyebrow. 'You know how they assess Elgar on the Continent, don't you?'

I was soon reduced to pulp.

'Right,' she said finally, smiling at my downcast face. 'I think you understand now the immaturity of your ideas, Eleanor. You sang "*Heidenröslein*" quite nicely in Wales; I think you should retain that, perhaps for your third song.' She seated herself at the piano. 'Let me hear you now.'

Pulped, I made a hash of it. I've always hated that song, anyway.

'You haven't practised,' she said accusingly. 'Again, please. Try to put more colour into your interpretation.'

Rebellion brought colour to my face at least, and more feeling to my voice; so I sang better and waited at the end for praise. She sighed, briskly shutting the piano.

'We must hope for the best, that's all. And you must try harder, for the school. Now go home and do your singing exercises. Cheer up, child, you won't be making the final decision.'

That was what I feared.

During the following week she buttonholed me before choir practice.

'Just glance at these, Eleanor.'

I glanced.

As I'd suspected, that wretched '*Heidenröslein*' was still there – but so was my beloved Mahler. I tried hard not to show my delight, in case she took it out again.

'But, Miss Armstrong, am I really to sing "Where Corals Lie" too? If I reach the semi-finals, mightn't they compare it unfavourably with the Schubert? *You* said – ' I risked – 'that they don't – er, appreciate Elgar on the Continent, and – '

'High time they learned. The song suits your voice, you know it well, which will be a help in public performance, and you sing it quite appealingly.' A darkening frown. 'I've spent time and effort on your entry, and we shall have to work hard before you're confident.'

'I know. Thank you, Miss Armstrong.' Having successfully taken her mind off '*Liebst du um Schönheit*' I beat a retreat to my place in the semi-circle of choir already forming at the far end of the room.

Mahler! Great.

Tommy tapped her music stand. 'Class! "Orpheus with his lute." Dan! Stop fooling around, remember you are playing for us. Iris! You're inclined to wander off the note, pay more attention. Ready, Dan? Keyboard fumbling helps nobody.'

We were full choir that day, and Tim Baskerville, my own particular friend, was just behind me. 'What's come over our Tommy?' he murmured later during a pause. 'Frost in summer, hm? Thwarted yearnings for Ruddigore?'

'Eleanor and Timothy, why are you not paying attention?'

'We were discussing a rather tricky point.'

'Really, Timothy? Which one?'

Tim stuttered out something about one of our entries for the Contest – 'Have you seen but a bright lily grow'. When Cassie Melford joined in I knew our necks were saved – she was Tommy's favourite, a vast pale stately prefect with a faultless memory for all kinds of music. The same could hardly be said of my best friend, Gina Morgan, who stood beside me in choir and often distracted me by making up strings of meaningless words when memory failed her. Several times Gina had been threatened with dismissal from the choir, but so far sheer talent had saved her.

'What was that you were singing?' Tim asked her during our tea-break. 'Why don't you read the words, ducky, if you're senile at sixteen?'

'I was just wondering why Cassie looks so like a whale, and then there I was, stuck, waiting for Tommy to strike me dead. The next thing I knew I was singing O so large, O so plain, O so pale is she.'

'Don't get thrown out, G.,' I begged. 'Not just before Austria. I'm sure we're getting a lecture on Good Behaviour Abroad from Tommy, any minute now.'

'Better still, Austrian behaviour.' Tim seized my hand and raised it ceremoniously to his lips.

'Hah, Baskerville! Practising continental manners, I see,' said Ruddigore's high-pitched voice, as he passed behind us, brushing against me with unnecessary force.

'Someone seems to be suffering from second spring,' murmured Dan Browning. 'Any buns left? You've swiped the lot, you greedy hogs.'

I shared mine with him, and he kissed my hand with a flourish.

'This sort of thing seems to be catching,' said Gina. 'Bet this year's choir sortie won't be quite so musically elevated as Tommy and Ruddigore are banking on.'

'You're right,' agreed Dan. 'Romantic backgrounds, richness of experience. Farewell buns and tea, welcome *Sachertorte*. Are you in trim for it, Nelly? Dewy English rose ripe for foreign plundering? In between Baskerville Hound's casual clutches?'

I laughed. 'Never thought of it like that – but I *am* singing "*Heidenröslein*". I don't know what sort of influence that will cast, if any.'

3

'Have a good time, my dear. Come back covered in laurels.'

My father stood on the station platform, looking solidly, dependably British in his dark suit. His rolled umbrella was crooked over his arm, his bowler hat tilted slightly towards his nose. In a shamefaced way I was glad my mother hadn't accompanied him. I didn't fancy trailing across Europe with tactless remarks about myself and my travelling companions ringing in my ears.

'Look after her, Tim, won't you?'

'He's not my nurse,' I said, outraged.

'Don't worry, sir.' Dan leaned from the window beside us. 'Baskervilles are ferocious watchdogs.'

'I'm sick of that joke, cut it out, can't you?' complained Tim.

Last-minute goodbyes were said, a whistle blew. A strong wind blew down the platform, enveloping us in hissing steam. I clutched at my school panama just as the train seemed to shake itself and glided with fierce puffings from the platform.

We waved, blew kisses. The station was retreating from us as though through the wrong end of a telescope. My father, leaning elegantly on his umbrella, grew smaller and smaller, half-veiled by mists of steam. There was a sudden sensation of leaving more behind me than the known and dear and everyday.

Dan and Tim were regarding me with masculine disapproval.

'These damn smuts.' I dabbed at my eyes, just as Miss Armstrong said frostily behind me, 'Eleanor, kindly take your seat farther along the train with the other girls.'

'Who needs Hound when they've got Bitch?' whispered Dan in my ear as I struggled past him. Tommy shepherded me along the corridor, scolding: 'I hope you're not going to make yourself conspicuous, Eleanor, you are one of our oldest girls. I should *not* have to remind you to set an example to the younger ones. Remember, while abroad we are all Ambassadors to another country – '

'Ambassadresses,' I murmured.

'What's that? So please behave as an Englishwoman should – neither pushing yourself forward nor giggling with boys, and keeping yourself neat and clean. When we leave Austria it may not be with honours but at least let it be said "They were such thoroughly nice English girls."' (I failed to imagine an equivalent phrase in German.) 'Now, here you are, Eleanor. Jessica! Move up into the corner seat, and make room. I am in the next compartment if anybody wants me.'

'She has a hope,' muttered Jess, as I took my seat between her and Gina.

'Look out, Nell. You've showered smuts all over me – you are a mucky creature,' said Cassie. We had a scratchy relationship always, partly caused by rivalry. She had the showiest contralto in the choir, I the best mezzo – and she had failed to get through the last soloists' heat.

'Sorry, Cass.' I stared past Jess at London suburbs retreating fast. Plumes of smoke blew between locomotive and townscape. Blue skies glimpsed between trees and roofs were ornamented with towering thunderlofts. My spirits began to rise. We were really away, not even Hitler would stop us now.

'Let's sing, shall we? Might as well, since we're all together.' And I began to croon: '"Thanks for the memory, of castles on the Rhine – "'

Cassie ostentatiously opened a magazine and began to

read as though she was in her room at home, not setting out on a journey that might change all our lives. Goodness, she was dull, I thought, as the train ran on, casting its shadow across sunlit patches of railway bank.

We were booked through to Innsbruck without stopover, on the night express from Paris, and all we got of the city's special flavour was an hour or two before changing stations for the next fourteen-and-a-half-hour stage of our journey.

Our younger choir members had couchettes, to prevent them getting overtired, though we older ones were expected to sleep sitting up, something I found almost impossible. This time I had a corner seat. For a while I read, then clicked off my lamp and sat staring out into the night as the express wound its way across Europe. I loved night travel: the track running through long stretches of dark woodland, stars seen between tossing branches and white smoke, lights pricking out, pale orange, from some isolated house or farm where the householders went late to bed, the steady climb towards higher altitudes – and watching wide rivers narrow to little milky streams in valleys far below.

Tonight my back was to the engine, so the whole land was flying away from me, and I felt a strong conviction that my schoolgirl life was flying with it like an unwinding ribbon while ahead lay an unpredictable future which would turn me into someone else.

Cassie's voice complained: 'That moonlight's on my face.'

Reluctantly I drew the curtain. Sometimes I dozed, to be jerked fully awake when the train stopped at Basle and a scurry of passengers left or boarded it. I woke again at Zurich, snuffed the chill mountain air, and felt my eyes gritty with tiredness. At seven we were all awake, hungry for breakfast in the restaurant car.

'Lovely, lovely Austria.' Gina slipped into the seat beside me. 'Lovely rolls and croissants and cherry jam. We don't 'arf look a set of crumpled English roses, Nell. Sing us *"Heidenröslein"*, to get us in the mood.'

And then at last we were gliding into Innsbruck. Immediately Bedlam broke loose: there were thirty-six of us, full choir, and the train corridor was jammed with thirteen-year-olds yelling for their baggage and seventeens trying to quell them, while above the din rose the desperate commands of Tommy and Ruddigore attempting to impose order on chaos. They might just as well have been wild geese honking overhead.

'Come on, G.,' I said. 'Let someone else cope.' I pulled my holdall off the rack, battered my way out between the juniors, and almost fell on to the platform. My hat was beneath my arm and my right pigtail had come undone, letting half my hair flow waterfall-loose, Lorelei fashion. Gina followed, dragging her own case. She looked peculiar too: she'd slept curled up with her cheek against an arm-rest which had left criss-cross marks on her face. We were first out of the train and quite unprepared for what happened next: the air was suddenly as full of song as a dawn chorus. Mozart greeted us, not risen from the grave but in the shape of a mixed choir, at least forty boys and girls singing away fit to bust. I dropped my bag with a thud on Gina's right foot.

'Ow, you clown, Nell. Gosh! Lord almighty –'

We stood staring. Behind us the juniors had hushed in equal amazement. This was when I really admired Tommy. I heard her say, 'Cassie, take over', and turned to see her step on to the platform, kick the door to behind her so that no one else could follow, and stand hands clasped, head slightly bowed, a gracious smile softening her features. When the Austrian choirmaster eventually turned to face us with a beaming smile she was clapping away genteelly with neatly-gloved hands. All along the train people were standing in the corridor clapping. The driver clapped, the guard clapped, G. and I clapped, softly, hoping no one would notice us.

'*Grüss Gott, meine Herrschaften*!' said the choirmaster when he could be heard. 'We wish you a happy stay.'

Tommy simpered a reply, managing at the same time to direct a disapproving glare towards Gina and me.

Luckily relief was at hand: that well-dressed, well-drilled choir broke rank. Shrilling noisy greetings it besieged our disembarking choir, yelling, waving bouquets, and even kissing Ruddigore as he alighted with Dan and Tim behind him. A dark girl with red ribbons threw her arms around Dan's neck, and a fat little blonde with a dimpling smile was pushing flowers through Tim's buttonhole.

They had mostly swept past me and Gina like the Severn Bore as I bent to recover my bursting holdall. A large brown hand gathered it up instead and a voice murmured in my ear, 'Allow me, Fräulein . . . and this is for you: take it, please?' A small stiff bouquet was pressed into my hands. Victorian, it looked: a frill of ribboned lace with the flowers frothing over it, their stems bound in silver, and at the centre one magnificent rose resting its petals on a cluster of deep-blue purplish gentians.

'Thank you,' I murmured, losing all my German. 'Oh, thank you very much.' I glanced back to see if Gina was all right, saw her rescued by a short fair boy with stocky shoulders, and thankfully followed my own rescuer to where some monster coaches were drawn up just outside the station.

'We will all go first to your *Gasthof* – so into the back of this one, please?'

He made me a little bow, standing aside for me to climb in first. Tim should see this, I thought, and made my way to the seats at the back, gingerly clasping my bouquet.

'Fräulein – '

'My name's Nell.'

Again, that little bow. 'Nell. I am Franz.' He flung my holdall up on to the rack and sat down beside me.

'Franz,' I repeated, looking down at the bouquet, and then up to find him watching me. I know people always use this cliché but it was like recognizing someone I had known all my life, and beyond.

'Nell,' he said again, smiling slightly. 'Do you always wear your hair so? I have never seen it so before.'

I laughed, breathlessly. 'One side came undone, that's all.' Dropping the bouquet in my lap I began replaiting.

'Perhaps you should wear it round your head, as do our girls?' He watched me thoughtfully.

'In my choir the rule is either pigtails – plaits, I mean – or short with a fringe.' He seemed puzzled. I drew a lock of hair across my forehead. 'Like this, see? Most of the little ones do that.' I was gabbling on, afraid of boring him. There was a short pause. Oh heavens.

But he didn't look bored. He was saying, 'You have seen the programme, Nell?'

'No, not the really official one.'

He searched his pocket, drew out some crumpled sheets of paper, and ran a finger down the first page. 'See? Your choir sing tomorrow.'

'Great. Tommy said we had all today free. And the soloists are the day after tomorrow.'

'So?' He frowned, and turned a page. 'I think this Tommy, he has it wrong. For some soloists sing today. This evening, or this afternoon.'

'Oh, Jemima!' A cold pit opened in the bottom of my stomach. 'Do they give names there?'

'Your school has someone in? Yes – she is here. Eleanor Dobell.'

'Me,' I said hollowly. My hands went hot and sticky. The long journey and little sleep had given me a dry throat. I felt both restless and exhausted. 'It's me, Nell. That's short for Eleanor. Lord – tonight.'

'Or afternoon.' He laughed.

'What's so funny? It's no joke.'

'It is not that – Nell. You must always your hair wear like Lorelei.'

'I didn't know Germans had a sense of humour,' I said rather crossly.

'They have not. Austrians do, and I am Austrian, and – ' He hesitated and didn't finish. At the time I barely noticed, I was too shattered by that first soloists' heat looming. Not surprisingly I felt the whole world had landed on my head. I buried my face in the bouquet as though it could help me escape to some safe garden paradise. The rose smelt like a briar. Warm, sweet and apple-y.

'Nell. I upset you, somehow?'

I shook my head.

'What is wrong, then?'

'Nothing. Everything. I don't know.' I looked at him helplessly, fearing amusement, but he seemed full of genuine concern. For a long moment we stared at one another. His right hand came down on mine. If anyone noticed us I didn't care.

'I will come and – and clap. If it is possible. My solos are today, too.'

I hoped he was feeling as breathless as I did, or perhaps he was simply quick off the mark with girls. I glanced at Gina, who was clutching the fair boy's bouquet. They weren't holding hands, though. I didn't know whether to leave mine where it was or withdraw it. Wouldn't that seem as if I made too much of it?

Our coach was filling up with the two choirs inextricably mixed. Ruddigore was on the front seat, Miss Armstrong just getting into the next coach with some juniors. Our cavalcade began to draw away from the station. Franz was still holding my hand as though he had every right to it.

'Please, Nell, may I show you Innsbruck? You like to sightsee?'

'I'd love that.' There was no need to say I'd been here before. 'Will we have much time, though?'

'We cannot sing all day. Besides, the instrumentalists take turn.'

'I know, but there's practice. And I'm in my choir. We shall be rivals.'

'Friendly rivals, I hope?'

'Of course.' I removed my hand at last, to retrieve my hat which had fallen on the floor; that wouldn't seem snubbing, surely.

Franz didn't look offended. I thought he was one of the most striking people I had ever seen, although not in a too glamorous or pretty-pretty way. An aquiline nose gave him a faintly haughty expression, which might not match his true nature – his mouth was too good-tempered and curled upward at the corners. I wondered how he saw me: comic, perhaps. Didn't foreigners usually find the English comic?

'How do you speak such good English, Franz?'

'My schooling was in Switzerland, where it is well taught. My father wished me to have languages, in case – ' I didn't learn why because just then the coach lurched to a halt before our hotel, and the Austrians' choirmaster appeared, shouting: 'Walter!'

Franz rose quickly, saying, 'That is for me. Herr Schmidt, *Ich komme.*'

'Walter? Not Franz?'

'Franz Felix Walter. You will like this *Gasthof*, Nell. It is *gemütlich*. I take your bag again?' He pulled it down and went ahead of me.

'Quick work,' hissed Gina in my ear, as we jostled off the coach together. 'I must say, he's marvellous-looking.'

Luckily Franz Felix Walter was now over on the other side of the yard, adding my holdall to the growing pile of luggage. Returning, he told me, 'This place does not take you all, the other *Gasthof* is nearby – we go there now. All soloists down at 14.00 to the Hall, so I see you then, Nell. And we speak more of this sightseeing?'

'Oh, yes.' My pulses leaped at the thought, although I tried for casualness: 'Thanks for carrying my case, and for the flowers. And the welcome!'

He smiled at me, indicated the waiting choirmaster, and loped off towards him.

We found Tommy in the *Gasthof* hall.

'Trust you two girls to arrive looking like vagabonds. Eleanor, you and Regina can share a room, no one else would stand it. And Eleanor, you had better have an immediate rest and then a very light meal. It's most unfortunate that you must sing today, or so Herr Schmidt tells me. Very bad of the Committee not to send the programme in advance.'

'Are Tim and Dan in this place?' asked Gina.

'*No*, Regina, they are not – just the girls. Even here, we must put three juniors to a room, and I must share with Cassie. A typical foreign muddle.'

Cassie didn't even look dismayed. I always thought there was something wrong with Prefects. 'Come on, G., let Tommy sign the register for us all,' I muttered. 'We'll go and snatch the best room we can find.'

We followed the porter upstairs and along the landing, passing a gigantic yellow porcelain stove. He was distributing cases, so we latched on to him, poking our noses into room after room until we found one at the back with splendid views and a balcony bearing pots of curly scarlet geraniums.

'Wow,' breathed Gina. 'Quick, stake your claim, Nell.' She flung her blazer on to one bed. 'Those two,' she directed the porter. 'That bag – and this case – *diese Käse* – '

'That's cheese, *Käse*,' I told her, and launched into my best show-off German. The porter smiled and relinquished our luggage. Other girls looked hopefully round our door but we shooed them out again. Cassie's voice said, 'Nell and Gina, this must be Miss Armstrong's room.'

'There's a larger one at the passage end, looks both ways – has its own shower, too.'

'Is there, G.? How did you know?' I asked, when Cassie had gone.

'Intuition. Quick, Nell! She said "rest", didn't she? Whip off your top and nip under that duvet-thing.'

I was stretched out flat beneath the quilt when footsteps

heralded Tommy's approach. I shut my eyes and breathed deeply.

'Oh, Miss Armstrong,' I heard Gina whisper, 'poor Nell was so exhausted, she's dropped straight off . . . I'm so sorry, we've started unpacking. Shall I wake her again? You're sure? Yes, it might be a pity. Sorry if we took the wrong room, I'm afraid Cassie thought the other had a shower . . . oh, thanks.'

The door shut. I sat up, stifling my giggles.

'I don't want to rest, I'm not sleepy. And I won't manage lunch later, I'd be sick.'

'I'll get you something light now.'

'Not if *diese Käse* is the best you can do.'

'Ungrateful beast. Just look at this lovely room I've got us. Think of playing Juliet to your Romeo on that balcony. Poor Tim will be playing Paris, I suppose.'

'Lay off, will you? I don't want your satiric eye on me all the time, thanks.'

'Poor Nell, you've got it fast and badly, haven't you? Like the plague. Never known you touchy before.'

I groaned, abandoning pretences. 'It's the last sort of thing I was expecting. How shall I manage if he's there watching me this afternoon?'

'He's probably thinking the same way. I'll come and support you too.'

I groaned again. 'My beastly butterflies are whirling. Wish we had nicer clothes. Hang my dress up for me, there's a love. Shake the creases out.'

That done, Gina took our phrasebook and went off in search of food. When she reappeared she was accompanied by a plump little waitress in Austrian costume who smilingly put a laden tray by my side.

'Danke schön.'

'Bitte schön, Fräulein.'

The tomato soup was thick and dark, spiced with herbs. Rolls were packed with pâté and cheese thick with caraway.

An enormous slab of Black Forest cherry cake was piled with cream.

I shuddered. 'I daren't – I couldn't. You have it, Gina.'

'Have the soup, and one of those rolls.' She began cramming food greedily into her mouth, talking indistinctly through it. 'Wonder where Tim and Dan are, hope their place is as good as this. Bet they'll be round shortly.'

I sipped the soup nervously. She watched me compassionately. 'Harden up, Nell. This is Life.'

'You sound like our gym mistress. That's worse than Tommy. Fish my music out, could you – I'll read it through again, before she scalps me.'

4

Some two hours later I stood before the long glass in our room, regarding myself critically. 'I look so schoolgirlish. It's these plaits. Did you see that girl in the hall with the French group? She was wearing make-up, lash stuff and all. I've brought a lipstick.' I dabbed it on my mouth and gazed doubtfully at myself. With those plaits it looked silly. Perhaps Franz wouldn't like it. I smoothed it in and bit my lips. Better. I rubbed some on my cheeks as well. 'Did you bring any scissors?'

'Only the nail sort.'

'Gimme, quick.'

Gina obeyed, and recklessly I chopped off one of my plaits.

'Nell.'

'Well, what?' I began sawing away at the other.

'You certainly look awful now. All mouth and eyes.'

'I thought of having a pageboy bob.'

'You're mad – you've only twenty minutes. You can't sing looking like that.'

I brushed out my hair and gazed at it hopelessly; it hung in zigzags. 'Help!'

'Help? You need a miracle.' But Gina shot from the room, while I regarded myself in dismay. Two or three minutes later she returned towing plump charming Anna who had brought my meal. She took one look at me and broke into laughter; then whisked away, to return shortly bearing a tray with larger scissors, hair clips, and setting lotion. She placed me before the glass and began work, deftly snipping, rolling my hair ends under, placing clips and applying strong-scented lotion. Gina watched us, awestruck.

'Hurry . . . make Anna cut you a fringe, or there'll be such a row.'

'I'd look awful,' I said stubbornly. 'What about that kind of all-round pageboy cut that Renaissance angels wear? Gimme a piece of paper, G.' I made a hurried sketch. 'Could you manage that?' I asked Anna. 'Were you ever a hairdresser?'

She nodded. 'Yes, I train, then I think to like hotel work better. Still many ladies ask my help. There – how is that now, Fräulein?'

I looked in the glass. 'Terrific. Thank you so very much, Anna.'

'It is nothing.' She began combing me out.

'It really suits you, Nell. You don't look like yourself at all,' said Gina.

'Thanks!' I pulled a face at her, wondering if Franz would approve my changed appearance. Too late to back out now, anyway.

Anna had already swept my hair clippings together, and now began helping me into my dress.

'Here comes Tommy,' breathed Gina. We both stood looking guilty, while Anna beamed with pride in her accomplishment. 'There, Fräulein!' She whirled about so that her dirndl stood out from her rounded figure, picked up her tray and, with a: '*Viel Glück*, Fräulein Nell' was out of the room before Tommy could speak.

I waited tensely while she looked me over. All she said was: 'Well, we can't alter it now. At least don't wear lipstick in the choir, Eleanor, and rub that colour off your cheeks, you look feverish. Are you ready?'

Down at the Hall we parted. Tommy joined the audience and those members of our choir including Tim and Gina who had come to give me moral support, while my accompanist Dan and I were led to the artists' room, where entrants from other countries looked us over appraisingly. I tried to control my breathing which didn't seem to be functioning.

'My hands are sweating, I'll hit dozens of wrong notes,' muttered Dan. I gave him a baleful look and turned my attention to the other competitors. As yet there was no sign of Franz, but he soon came in, looking searchingly about him. When he saw me his smile was one of faint amusement as he took in my changed appearance. I felt myself go pink as any *Heidenröslein*, but the warmth of his greeting reassured me. My diaphragm relaxed, now even public disaster wouldn't matter – nothing would be changed between us, I knew it with a curious certainty that belied my inexperience.

That afternoon four other people sang before me. With an effort I turned my thoughts away from Franz and listened to what was happening beyond the curtain. Two of the singers struck me as outstanding. If any who had sung that morning, or would sing that evening, were as good, I didn't rate my chances high.

'Eleanor Dobell. England.'

'We're on,' said Dan, and I preceded him to the dais, Franz encouraging us with a thumbs-up as we passed. Somehow my wobbly legs supported me. The Hall looked terrifyingly large, with only a quarter of it full and the Adjudicators lodged far off on the balcony.

Dan crossed to the piano while I stared grimly into the middle distance, fearing my face muscles would set like plaster. It seemed ages before his first notes sounded – fortunately as firm and clear as water, giving me no excuse to muff my entrance, although my voice sounded strange to me in this strange hall, and a bit unsure:

Liebst du um Schönheit,
O mich nicht liebe!
Liebe die Sonne,
sie trägt ein goldenes Haar!

Liebst du um Jugend,
O mich nicht liebe!

Liebe den Frühling,
der jung ist jedes Jahr!

Liebst du um Schätze,
O mich nicht liebe!
Liebe die Meerfrau,
sie hat viel Perlen klar!

Liebst du um die Liebe,
O ja, mich liebe!
Liebe mich immer,
dich lieb ich immer, immerdar!

At the song's end there was real applause, though I was sure I'd missed the poetic subtlety of the Mahler. Still, now warmth had been established between me and the audience I could launch myself more confidently into the gentle lulling opening of 'Where Corals Lie'. Just as in the song, the music lured me, lured me – my voice opened up, and I felt the same thrill in singing as I felt when riding a galloping horse. In fact, I was almost run away with, 'to rolling worlds of wave and shell', onwards to the last beseeching 'leave me, leave me, let me go, and see the land where corals lie'.

Then it was over. Dan and I were taking our bow together, and I was unsure if the rustling in my ears was applause or my heart gone crazy. He grinned at me as we made our exit. 'Well? What d'you think?'

'Dunno.' I felt emptied of feeling. 'What did it sound like?'

'All right. I was busy concentrating. Cripes, Nell – you fairly let yourself go in "Corals"!' His glance flicked wickedly to Franz, who came up to put his hands on my shoulders and give me a small friendly shake.

'*Ausgezeichnet*, Nell! It enchanted.' An odd, considering look. 'Something very strange about it, though – '

'About my singing? You don't surprise me.'

'*Nein, nein* – only about your choice. You will see, later.' He nodded mysteriously.

It was a while before his turn came. We sat around on hard chairs, among people who had sung already and those who bit their nails beforehand. Franz sat in silence, concentrating till his name was called. I spent the time wondering what he'd meant.

'Franz Walter, Osterreich.'

He got up and stalked past me unseeingly, followed by his accompanist, the short fair boy called Peter who had chatted to Gina on the coach.

There was a brief silence, then the first plaintive phrases of the introduction sent a tingling sensation of shock down my spine. I sat with my hands clasped tight together, waiting for the voice's entry; Franz's voice, singing with compelling sadness a song that had been so much a part of me this summer –

Ich bin der Welt abhanden gekommen –

'I have become a stranger to this world.' The last of the five Rückert songs in the Mahler cycle; the one that follows '*Liebst du um Schönheit*'. It seemed uncanny, and exactly right; my choice was strange, as he had said – and yet – could anything be stranger than our meeting, and the chance that had brought us here together?

Ich bin gestorben dem Weltgetummel –

I am dead to the tumult of this world,
My resting place is one of quietness.
I live alone in my heaven,
In my loving, in my song.

Something about Franz's singing of it sent further shivers down my spine. The whole spirit of the song was there. It was as though he was creating a space around him, a shell. I did not know if I was included there.

He had finished. Peter played the last bars. A second silence was followed by rapturous applause, the most so far for anyone.

Peter began to play again. The light, rapid hoofbeat rhythm of '*Abschied*'.

'"*Ade! du muntre, du fröhliche Stadt, ade!*"' sang Franz joyfully, with certainty and flourish, yet infusing the song with the nostalgia of the departing rider. The maturity and contrast of his interpretations made me uneasy – my first love was some rare phoenix, competition for him must be fierce. And my stay here in Austria was so short.

Again a hush fell in the Hall, to be broken by frenzied continuous applause for an accomplished performance that was more than accomplishment, an elusive quality of something larger than ourselves. Dan whispered in my ear, 'No doubt about that.' All the comments near us were favourable. Only I sensed a touch of hidden coldness, which was not like jealousy, for the praise was there all right.

Franz and Peter rejoined us, both flushed and relaxed by success. I stood up, and Franz and I held hands, smiling into each other's eyes, oblivious of other people.

'But Franz – the Mahler – ' I stammered out.

'I know,' he said gravely.

We were feeling the same way, an almost superstitious awe at what had happened.

Dan broke the spell, clapping Franz heartily on the shoulder. 'Super, we thought. Didn't we, Nell?'

'Super? More than. They couldn't fault you, not anywhere.'

He was still looking at me, still holding my hands. He shrugged. 'You think so, but – There is always "but". You wish to stay, Nell?'

'I? Don't we have to?'

'No, we can return to listen later, this evening and for the results. A few more people sing now. Come out with me.'

'We can leave, just like that?' My heart was batting like mad.

'But certainly. There is a back way out.'

I hesitated. Dan knew what was on my mind. He gave me a friendly push. 'You go, Nell. I'll tell Tommy you needed some fresh air. Good for the lungs, you know.'

'I couldn't have sat there a moment longer. Could you?'

We stood outside the Hall, breathing deeply in the sunlight. The blood tingled in my veins, I wanted to run and yell and dance.

Franz made no reply. He was looking away from me along the street. Although we weren't even touching, I sensed his tension.

'Quickly, *komm*', cross here – ' He seized my arm and hustled me across the road. 'This way, to the river, down this street.'

Meekly, I obeyed. He was almost dragging me, and a feeble protest went unheard. Perhaps I should have kept my plaits, wound them round my head and said nothing but 'Yes, Franz' and 'You're always right'. I pulled rather sharply away.

'Need we almost run?'

'I am sorry, you do not understand. There were some people coming. I did not want them to – to insult you, or push you around.'

We had reached the river bank and I stopped in my tracks.

'Push me! Why ever should they? Is that how they treat strangers now in Austria?'

'It is who you walk with. . . . And you are the last person I would wish to harm.'

'Harm? What harm could you do me? Who are those people? Why would they hurt anyone? They looked just a bunch of boys. Scouts or something.'

'Nell, once I too a Scout was. I left, because I could not the – the hypocrisy, you say? – bear. You see, Scouts have changed here. Always there is one troop for Jews – and two Aryan boys must join to make things look better. In all other troops not one Jew may join. There is no pretence of free choice left.'

I must have shown my bewilderment, for he added, 'Nell, did you not know I am a Jew? Half one, anyhow.'

'I didn't even think of it. Why ever should I? You can't believe it would have made a difference.'

'One gets accustomed to it making differences.' He sounded humble. I couldn't bear him to sound like that, specially not after his triumph in the Hall. I put both my hands over his and held them hard.

'You mustn't let them make you mind, ever. Not ever, do you hear?'

He relaxed then; he even laughed. 'Dear Nell, how good to hear you angry. For me.'

'Think how they applauded you,' I urged.

'Oh yes. Then they were pleased. After all, they are still musical.' He spoke without arrogance, just a nice sense of his own worth. 'Probably some already regret. The marks will show.'

I recalled the odd chill behind the praise in the artists' room. Outside, the sun still shone, but that remembered chill now touched me. 'I didn't know things were like that here. Only in Germany.'

'You are so – innocent.' He hesitated on the last word, and I guessed that he'd meant to say 'ignorant'.

Ignorant I was, too. My own fault entirely, drifting along in a musical haze, not doing my homework about the conditions in Austria. How often my father had spoken of European affairs while I closed my mind mulishly, afraid he was leading up to a ban on the whole Contest.

'Please, Franz, explain. Tell me how things are.'

'And spoil your holiday – your festival? And how can you truly understand what happen here?' The sad dignity of his words opened an abyss between us.

'I want to understand. I must know how things are for you. Do you think I want to go home saying, "I had a lovely time" and just forget or ignore things that sound so – so evil?' I had to make him understand that in companionship we had come a long way already from the pretty platform greetings, the morning songs and bouquets.

He leaned his elbows on the parapet and stared bleakly across the water.

'Franz?'

'There is much. Why trouble *you* with such things?'

'Because you're you, and I'm me, and though we only met this morning – ' My hands gripped his arm, almost shaking it. He turned to look at me.

'Nell,' he said. It was enough. He put his arm around my shoulders. We stood silent for some minutes till he released me, turning his back to the parapet, and murmured: 'I should be watching for who comes.'

'As bad as that?'

'Twice – three times so bad.'

'But *these* people?'

'Are more anti-Jewish often than the Germans themselves. At least, some. Will they not be happy when Hitler walks in and they can fall on us! Hitler, their Austrian-born Führer.'

I felt crushed by things beyond my comprehension. Here was the sun shining down on Innsbruck and the serene snow-capped peaks, and on family parties strolling in the sunshine, out to enjoy themselves. Yet beneath it all ran this dark undercurrent that made Franz turn from the sun-gilded river so that he could . . . watch.

'Of course, even some Austrian Nazis do not want the *Anschluss*,' Franz was saying. 'They want only power for themselves, they have just sense enough to see they would not keep it under Hitler. This type want Austria free, yet Nazi. Fools! The very worst pro-German Nazis will win.'

'How can you be so sure? Many people will fight it, surely.'

Franz's smile was bitter. 'We are so optimist – in so pessimist way. We shall slide on and on hoping for the best to happen. And it will not, Nell. And as for us Jews . . . ' He paused, then added, 'I am only half-Jewish, through my father.'

'Then – '

'Oh, half is enough,' he said impatiently. 'Although my father is no practising Jew, you understand. It is sad, Nell, how we all saw – no, see ourselves as Austrian. Austria is our country too. It breaks the heart to know what happens here. I am glad my mother is dead. Think! Now Mussolini has his pact with Hitler Austria is like a nut between nutcrackers. Any day, the crunch. The rest of Europe will remember us when it is threaten too. But then, is too late.'

It was like crossing a green flowery meadow to find oneself looking over the edge into a slimy pit. Hell so near. What childish pride and joy I had been taking in my pathetic musicianship when this – this – Why, it was grotesque that Franz could sing in the contest to wild applause and stand half an hour later with his back to the river watching for enemies.

'Why must it be like this? It's disgusting. It – it makes me want to kill them all.'

Some of the misery left Franz's face. He even laughed. 'Good, Nell. I will provide a list. But you ask me why this should be? There are too many of us here in Austria. Specially Vienna felt swamped by refugees from Eastern pogroms. Always, we were driven west. And often we do so well; this, they cannot forgive. Then up rises this foul Nazi breed, with their mad doctrine of pure Aryan blood. Beasts, banned till Dollfuss died, and then out of hiding they come. Was always some anti-Jewishness here, but now, in just four years . . . You will not understand, you are English.'

Vague memories of historic persecutions came to me. Early horrors in York. Protestants burned by Mary Tudor's orders. Catholics killed in Elizabeth's reign. And the murder of the Flemish weavers. Could that sort of thing lurk in us still?

'I'm glad you told me,' I said. 'And I do understand. It's vile for you, and for your father too.'

'Schatz,' he murmured. *'Ich hab' dich gern*. Never will I forgive me if you face horrors while you stay. I should not have said, come out with me.'

Could *'Ich hab' dich gern'* really mean what I thought it did? I said almost fiercely, 'Franz Felix Walter, I'd never have forgiven you if you hadn't. Just for this afternoon, let's try to forget the horrors, shall we? Weren't you going to show me your town? Come on, then. And if things get too bad here you and your father must come to England. Perhaps you could even stay with us till – till things get better.'

It sounded simple enough, though Franz shook his head and smiled. He took my hand again and walked me off towards the Maria-Theresian-Strasse and the Old City. But he did say one thing that should have warned me: 'My father will not believe the *Anschluss* could happen. And what he will not believe, and while he stays . . .' He sighed, and left it there.

5

In spite of everything we managed to enjoy the sightseeing. Franz parted from me at my *Gasthof*, where I received a heavy scolding from Tommy before dinner.

'Really, Eleanor, you look exhausted. You should not have gone out without permission, as you well knew, particularly as you missed hearing the other singers. Kindly remember you are my responsibility, and I must learn more about this young Walter before I agree to your spending more time alone with him. Understand me, if there's cause to complain of your conduct you will go straight home.'

'I'm truly sorry, Miss Armstrong.' But I knew the thrill of underlying happiness didn't escape her all-seeing eye.

She snorted. 'Immature girls always think Austria's romantic, it goes straight to their heads. Now go and change for dinner, and brush that stupid hairstyle into some sort of shape. You will sit by me in the Hall this evening, and stay until the end. Even if you've failed today it's grossly discourteous to the Adjudicators to do otherwise.'

I escaped upstairs. Gina was sitting on our balcony, twirling a geranium bud between her fingers and studying a phrase book.

'Hi, ducky, where did you get to? Don't say, I can guess. Dreamy, isn't he? Tommy's waiting to give you a right pasting.'

'She has. What are you mugging up?'

She sighed. 'Small talk for Peter. He's not quite Franz-standard, I know. Still, he does look a bit like Schubert. And we can't all clasp the top soloist to our bosoms in half an hour.'

'Peter looks about thirteen,' I said tactlessly, looking for my dressing-gown.

'He's eighteen in September, and just as bright as your chum in his own way. And since they're friends we'll make a nice foursome.'

But my mind was on twosomes. I said sourly, 'It will be fivesomes if Tommy can manage it.'

'Oh, Tommy! Wait till she meets some dried-up musicologist and starts tea-dancing to the strains of the "Kaiserwaltz".'

'Some hope.' I picked up my sponge and towel and headed for the bathroom.

The last group of that day's singers had been summoned for eight o'clock – or twenty hours, Continental time. Down at the Hall I settled meekly in the seat on Tommy's right. Franz with his choirmaster, was some rows ahead, and didn't seem to be watching out for me, or so I thought. I was wearing the rose from my morning bouquet, hoping that Tommy would believe it was in tribute to Schubert and '*Heidenröslein*'. Now I wondered if it was too forthcoming of me or even, dreadful thought, coy. I pushed it beneath my collar.

Gina, Tim and Dan were with us, Tommy having left Cassie behind in charge of the others. I could feel Gina stifling yawns behind me while a tall Spanish mezzo sang '*Du Ring an meinem Finger*' with some simpering glances at her hand. Tommy had always dinned into me that acting while you sing is a subtle art, and straightforward interpretation better than the wrong sort of mime.

The last of the singers was a bunchy little German from Munich, a true Hitler-*Mädchen* type, with hair plaited into shells above her ears. A lovely voice though: high and pure as a choirboy's, and she knew how to use it too.

'One for the finals, I bet,' hissed Gina in my right ear, and I heard Tommy murmur something approvingly to Ruddigore.

Fat little Irma Braun took her bow and departed. Then one of the Contest's organizers took her place on the dais to make a short speech in German, French and English. Other foreigners evidently had to make do with that. He finished by telling us that the Adjudicators would take an hour for refreshment and then give their decisions. In the meantime a buffet supper was awaiting us on the terrace.

Gina came instantly alive like a young owl at twilight.

'Thank God it's not all too earnest. Come on, let's go and find our chums.' She dragged me from my seat and hustled me down the aisle before Tommy could start marshalling us together. I hung back a little. Gina wasn't serious about Peter, which was why she didn't mind what he might think. But I didn't want Franz to feel I was pursuing him like an ardent rider to hounds (though such an English simile would hardly have occurred to him).

Under Gina's masterful guidance Franz and I were soon forging our way out towards the lantern-lit terrace. I was remembering Tommy's warnings; still, even she could hardly describe this well-peopled terrace as somewhere I was alone with him. Peter and Gina were well ahead, though, chatting together in an atrocious mixture of languages, while Franz kept silence. I could sense some constraint, some holding back, and wondered how to approach this suddenly confusing stranger. When he spoke, abruptly, it was about Gina.

'Your friend – she seems a very happy person.'

'Gina? I don't think she's exactly happy. She's got a shouting, roaring father, and a fretty sort of mother. But Gina says life is for living, and you must never let other people spoil it for you.'

Franz nodded, said, 'So!' and lapsed into another brooding silence.

That afternoon I, at least, had been wildly, sweetly happy. Tonight it was down to earth with a bang as Franz walked beside me, hands deep in his pockets as though deliberately cutting all communication. His profile, etched against lantern-light, reminded me of an offended eagle, solitary on some high perch.

Suddenly I felt furious with him. 'Franz, you're really impossible.'

'I am – why?'

I turned aside, unable to express myself. We were close to the supper table now, at the edge of the terrace.

'Let's have some wine, anyway.' I would have drunk an entire bottle, to break this sense of isolation. He was examining the labels.

'This one is a good wine.' He raised his own glass and said formally, as though I were a stranger, '*Prost*.'

As I drank, my hand brushed aside my collar and revealed the rose in all its full-blown glory, slightly crushed.

'Why do you hide the rose, Nell – since you wear it at all?' His voice had softened.

I looked down into my glass, and murmured, 'Tommy. She might have objected.' Then I risked the truth. 'I looked for you in the hall, but you seemed – not to notice.'

'Dear, dear Nell. I smiled at you when you came in but *you* did not seem to see! Then I am thinking: of course, she does not really wish for friendship with – with a – someone like me.'

'You thought that of *me*?'

'Forgive, Nell. Please. I am sorry, so sorry. Of course you are not like that. It is just I am thinking, maybe someone says – things – and – '

'So am I sorry! And horrified. That someone like you could feel – no, it's horrible.'

Now I could almost hear my mother's voice, warning me against ever showing my feelings outright. ('And above all, Nell, never let them know you care too much.') But Franz and I might have so little time together, and anyway how could one apply those arid principles of hers to a situation like this one?

'You've made me miserable tonight, Franz. Don't ever say

anything like that again, do you hear? If a silly little misunderstanding is going to make you cut right off, what would happen with a larger one?'

'I would never make you miserable, if I could help it.' He took my hand and kissed it, not mockingly as Tim or Dan would have done. Then he rearranged the drooping rose beneath my collar. Suddenly I remembered the fat little German girl's serene sexless voice singing *'Heidenröslein'*, and I shivered.

'But what is wrong now?'

'Nothing . . . just something silly. I thought of Irma Braun singing *"Heidenröslein"*. It's such a sad song, so – so ill-omened. Sometimes I've thought – if you wallow in tragedy – you could – can bring it about.' Tears pricked my eyes. 'I wish Tommy hadn't picked it for me,' I blurted out. 'I'm sure it's unlucky.'

'But what is this, now? You must believe that you will win. Tell yourself, I reach the final – I, Nell Dobell.'

'That's not what I meant, at all. Anyway, is that what you'll tell yourself?'

'Not so.' He fingered the rose's petals again. 'I say: by grace of God and if no one is too afraid of someone else, then to the next heat I through am.'

'Oh, Franz! You turn your English back to front when you're upset, did you know? And isn't it just too easy, living in this atmosphere, to imagine bad things round every corner?'

He sighed, and shook his head. 'If *"Heidenröslein"* is unlucky, that rose – our rose – looks like all luck and happiness. Keep it safe for us, Nell.'

'I'll always keep it.'

We stood looking at one another. It was like the afternoon, all over again –

A hand gripped my shoulder.

'Hi, there, you two.' Tim was grinning down at me. 'Dan and I have been looking for you and Gina – you shot from the hall like rabbits escaping from a gun.'

The precious moment was destroyed. 'Go and find her then,' I snapped at poor Tim. 'She's with Peter.'

'But it wasn't Gina I really wanted. Come on, Nell, introduce me, won't you?'

Damn Tim, for not taking a hint. 'Tim Baskerville – oh, and Dan Browning. Franz Walter.'

'I remember – you sang rather well, Walter. And you seem to have impressed our Nellie. Dan and I are coming to hold her hand for the results.'

'She will succeed,' said Franz equably. 'And I will hold her hand.'

Dan laughed. 'Sabres for two. Or is that just at Heidelberg?'

'It is not Austrian, that. Here, by the lake, we may just break each other the nose, yes?'

Franz looked so belligerent and Tim so comically ruffled that I said hurriedly, 'No, don't break each other the nose, that's silly. Please both of you calm down. Tommy's already threatened once to send me home.'

'Only a passing thought of Dan's, brought on by the night and the music,' said Tim quite amicably. 'Walter, we'll lend you Nellie. She's coming back to England, anyway.'

'Nobody lends me. What's got into you Tim? That wine, I should think. I'm having supper with Franz now, so see you both later.'

I glared so fiercely at Tim and Dan that they retreated in search of Gina. Franz was still looking slightly put out. 'So! Good chance I catch you on the station platform, yes?'

'Tim's just an old friend, so is Dan.' ('Don't always be so devastatingly candid, Nell,' my mother would have said.) 'Our school's co-ed, that's boys and girls together. So we see a lot of each other, joint activities. That's all.'

'I am glad,' said Franz simply. 'Now shall I feed you well, before we face the lions in the Hall?'

A banquet was what we really needed that night. Even without it we did well enough, working our way through the display of food. Regretfully I gave one last lick to a sumptuous ice.

'Finished? Come, Nell – just time to show you the lake.'

We ran down the terrace steps. There was a slight ground mist; the lake itself was a gentle silver sheen reflecting cloud and sky and moonlit mountain peak. Beneath a giant cedar's indigo shade Franz stopped and pulled me into his arms. Of course it was far from the first time I'd been kissed, but never before like that. My whole body throbbed with pleasurable excitement unguessed at even in my most imaginative moments. Till then kisses had been a sop to vanity, nothing more, sometimes even boring.

'Franz,' I murmured, when I could speak again. I wanted to say, 'Never stop,' but something, probably my upbringing, prevented me.

'*Geliebte*, Schatz.' He held me closer, burying his face in my hair. 'Forget, please Nell . . . forget me.' All the time he was clutching me so fiercely that obeying would have been impossible, even if I'd wanted to.

'But Franz, what is it, what's wrong – why should you want me to forget you?'

'It is the future. What comes to us here – to the world.'

All at once the lantern-light looked pitifully faint against the growing darkness and oily mists writhing upward from the lake. Words read only this summer in my English class came vividly to my mind, and I shivered.

'Nell? Is it what I said?'

'Yes . . . and something I learned, once.'

'Tell me.' He took my face between his hands, and when I hesitated insisted, 'Yes, Nell. Anything you think is important to me too.'

Looking over his shoulder at the lake's faint shining I quoted reluctantly: '"Finish, good Iras, the bright day is done, and we are for the dark".'

He stood silent, still holding me.

'Dear Franz, come to England!' I said urgently. 'And stay for – for – ' For ever, I meant, but changed to, 'It's what your father must want for you. Isn't it?'

'And leave him here – to face what comes, alone?'

'Why shouldn't he come too?'

'Nell, you do not know him, or understand. Not speak of these things now. It waste our time, our little, little time.'

Some minutes later a bell summoned us back to the Hall. Hand in hand we went to join the jostling crowd making its way towards the entrance. Just before we reached it the jostling turned to rougher horseplay. A girl cried out shrilly. Someone gave a high jeering laugh. Franz urged me forward, and was thrown hard against the doorpost. I struck backward with my elbow and was kicked on the shin by what felt like a hobnailed boot. I turned, raging, to find three crophaired louts beside us.

'Stop that!' I yelled, forgetting my German. They laughed, and one of them growled out, *'Des Juden Mädchen.'*

Franz brought his fists up, and I cried out, 'Oh *no*,' pushing myself between him and our attackers.

'Out of the way, Nell!' He tried to struggle back past me but I wouldn't – and couldn't – move from where I was. One of the brutes leaned forward and spat accurately into Franz's face. I wriggled round, and managed to bring my knee up hard where it would hurt most. Just in time to avoid real bloodshed an authoritative voice rang out from the rear, too fast and gutterally for me to understand, except by the sudden cowing of our tormentors, who hung back as Franz and I were swept to safety by the inflowing crowd. Expressionless, he wiped the spittle from his face.

'Nell, you are not hurt?' His voice was unsteady.

'No,' I lied. 'Those brutes, they don't belong in *here*, do they?' He shook his head. His pallor scared me. 'Let's find ourselves seats, shall we, Franz?'

Tommy would throw fits if I didn't home straight to her side, but after that nasty little scene I didn't care. We found ourselves places in the third row, and as we sat down I murmured low in his ear, 'They picked on us specially. On you, I mean. I was just incidental.'

'Yes, I was warned. But I am not expecting anything from the garden side.'

'*Warned*?'

'Not to sing here – not to enter as soloist, I mean. *Natürlich*, I will no notice take.'

'But Franz! There are all the finals still to come!'

'Please, Nell – do not worry. You see, I will not reach the finals, anyway. And they surprised us, in that crush. With fists I am good, believe me.'

'Be as good as you like, but – eight fists against two? And those beasts wore vicious boots.'

'But how – they kicked *you*? Did they? Nell, I will wring their necks one by one, it is a pleasure.'

'Hush, they didn't. I saw. And here come the Adjudicators. Franz, don't make things harder for yourself,' I whispered. 'I'm quite all right, really. But I'm afraid for you – you're bound to reach the finals, you're far and away the best singer I've heard.'

'Perhaps. But it is only because Herr Schmidt is a good fellow, and stubborn, that I still sing in our choir.'

On the dais someone was now booming out messages of goodwill to the contestants generally. Such a pity that everyone couldn't be a winner and yet – beam – each entrant here was among the select group of winners from their own land, which should not be forgotten since we come together to make and listen to music, not simply to compete. And blah-blah-blah –

The list of successful singers was in alphabetical order. Soon my name was called. But I was on tenterhooks still: not wanting Franz hurt by failure, nor wishing him more endangered by success.

' . . . Frederica Varviso, Astrid Vandervelde, Franz Walter.'

There was a lot of clapping. Franz was still pale, though smiling, and the unsuccessful soloists tried to hide their disappointment. As we all rose to leave I was almost reeling with exhaustion; more had been packed into that one day than into any ordinary two years. I was even relieved to find Tommy at our side, come to reclaim her lost lamb from the ravening Austrian wolf. Stumbling over the names, I introduced them. Tommy, being Tommy, came straight to the point.

'If you're to continue seeing this girl I shall want a word with your choirmaster. Over supper he somehow –' sniff – 'eluded me. You understand, young man, that I am *in loco parentis* regarding Eleanor?'

It was too shamingly Mrs. Gaskell. Suppose Tommy scared Franz off? Suppose Herr Schmidt hinted at the dangers of being Jewish? Even if he weren't anti-Semitic he might think it his duty to warn her.

'Certainly, Fräulein. I will advise Herr Schmidt you wish to speak with him tomorrow, yes?'

Tommy looked at Franz thoughtfully. I could see he had risen in her estimation. 'That will do nicely. Now come along, child, you should be in bed.'

I followed her, yawning. At the top of the aisle I looked back. Franz still stood where we'd left him, smiling. He waved. I breathed a sigh of relief. Probably he just saw Tommy as a typically dotty English spinster.

'Great, your getting through, Nell,' said Gina, burrowing into her pyjamas. She seemed very wide awake. 'Hope you heard us cheering, or were you only thinking of the boyfriend? Peter's a lamb, though he hasn't got those heroic sort of looks. We can have a great time here in spite of Tommy, what do you think?'

'Nothing. Too tired.' I stripped off my clothes and got into bed, pulling the duvet up over my ears. Then I remembered the rose and dragged myself up again to put it lovingly in water.

'All this "Go, lovely rose" stuff! You've both got it badly.' Gina eyed me with amused sympathy.

'Shut up, can't you?'

I flumped back into bed and lay willing myself to sleep. Instead I kept wondering if Franz had got home safely or if the hobnailed brigade had been keeping watch. When I slept at last my dreams were full of darkness. Scudding clouds twisted into rose-like circles, were blown before a rising gale, their petals torn away and shaped into gleaming metal swastikas. Through it all my father's anxious voice kept saying, 'If you'll only promise to be sensible, Nell . . . be sensible.'

6

Next day I woke lighthearted, as though all my worries had been dreamed away. I felt full of energy, really alive. After all, Innsbruck was one of my favourite places, and this time it was shared with Franz.

'Must you stay glowing in that bed forever?' asked Gina. 'Staring crazily before you, not hearing a word I say?'

'Sorry. Just look where we are, Gina – look at the sun on that mountain.'

'I know. I'd like to go and climb it right now, before breakfast. Or perhaps cable car, after lunch.'

'Choir heat this morning, anyway. Maybe we won't be free.' I got out of bed. 'But if I am – why then – '

'Why then: "Romeo, Romeo, wherefore art thou Romeo" – mmm?'

'Oh, come on, G. Breakfast.'

It was while we were dressing that I told her of the attack on Franz. She gave a longdrawn whistle. 'How frightful. Truly, Nell, should you get mixed up with this? Your bruise looks bad enough.'

'I can't help being mixed up with it. And I'm not making terms, but I'm scared Austria may. Gina, suppose something happens so that they close their frontiers? Then I must stay here, somehow.'

She whistled again. 'And would you really?'

'Yes, if he wants me.'

'Well, you couldn't, you're under age still. So's he, I imagine. And neither of you earning anything! Is his father well off?'

'Dunno. It will work out, it must. Oh, G., say it will. Make me feel it.'

'All right, honey child. It will.' She sounded unconvinced.

I sighed. 'I never guessed love was such hell. At least some people at home don't believe Hitler will go on marching forever.'

'Mmmm. Thank God at least for those delicious rolls and black cherry jam we get here. Hurry, Nell. Someone else will get our share.'

The coach came soon after breakfast, collecting our full choir. Tim sat beside me.

'How's Count Dracula? Got any toothmarks yet to warn other people off, Nell, sweet Nellie, divine and sought-after Eleanor?'

'So funny, aren't you?'

'The Teutonic tribes are said to have no humour. Even Count Drac's dark passionate glances aren't food for mirth? He does "*Küss die Hand*" quite beautifully doesn't he? Our Dan is proving clairvoyant.' Tim caught up my right hand and licked it.

I withdrew it smartly. 'Clown-dog. Study your music.'

'Hey, what's going on?' asked Dan from the seat behind us.

'I'm protesting about being cast off for a dark stranger. We don't want these sinister foreign chaps getting hooks on our girls. Don't worry, Nell, your virtue's safe, we're both ready to inflict duelling scars on said Drac while you swoon in the shade.'

'You stick to school games, Tim, safer for little boys. Thank God, here's the Hall.'

In the foyer we milled around waiting for Tommy's shepherding. I began studying some notices pinned to a blackboard. Without turning round I knew who was standing at my elbow.

'Nell.'

'Franz. You got home safely – nobody followed?'

He smiled down at me. Oh God, I thought. When he does that I'm lost. 'No, I was with friends. Our local Nazis are only brave in numbers. I saw you come in just now. Your feathers – someone ruffle them, yes?'

'So you noticed?'

'I notice everything about you,' he said simply.

It was a wonder to me that two people could be so close that nothing one felt could be missed by the other. In a way it was scaring. How could this happen to me, who hadn't wished for nor expected it, who would have told anyone a week ago that it only happened on the flicks or in Shakespeare as quoted by Gina – and he was writing of another time, when most things happened more intensely, at an earlier age.

'One of my friends had been ribbing me.'

'Ribbing?'

'Teasing.'

A sidelong glance. 'About me?' He looked pleased.

'Yes.'

'Well, it is obvious.'

'What, though?'

'That we love.'

Tears started to my eyes. Oblivious of everyone else, Franz put his arm around me. 'One day we are together always, Nell. We will marry, yes?'

'Oh, yes! Yes, Franz.'

'In spite of everything,' he said fiercely. 'This I promise you.'

'Then if Hitler invades, will you come to England?'

'And if I could not – would you come here?'

'Of course,' I said; knowing the difficulties would be insuperable, driving myself to believe that we could surmount them if I said so firmly enough.

'But we dream. It would be impossible,' said Franz sadly.

'Don't say that. Never say it.'

We both stared at the notices as though somewhere among them was an answer to all our problems. Presently Franz said: 'See, there is a concert this afternoon, free, for us all. But for us I have a better idea: a trip to the mountains. Will you come?'

'Lovely . . . but, oh dear, I'll have to ask Tommy.'

'The duenna.' He grinned. 'She does not pass me as suitable?'

'We'd have heard soon enough if you weren't! She might think we twist her arm rather.'

'Which means?'

'Oh, putting on pressure too fast. And not being serious enough about music. It might be easier to wangle it tomorrow.' I knew Tommy so well and he didn't. I hoped he wouldn't find my caution detestable.

'You mean, today you should either be here with other singers, or at this concert. Nell, whatever you want, I too. It is like that between us.'

'And for me, always.' I breathed a sigh of relief. 'Look, Franz, did you see this too – about the annual Wagner festival at Bayreuth? This year the Wagner family are donating tickets for a lottery,' and I read out the English translation: "Soloists who reach the semi-finals are eligible to enter the draw for opera tickets". Bayreuth!' I added yearningly. 'What a chance.'

'So. And you would take it?' Franz was looking at me rather darkly.

'I'm crazy about that music,' I said hungrily, yet a bit on the defensive. 'Of course I know Wagner was – was quite anti-Semitic, and wrote some very insulting things about the Jews, but he couldn't guess Hitler was coming after him, could he?'

Franz gave a wry smile. 'No. Though that do not excuse the things he wrote. It is unfortunate when a great man writes so. Because he was remarkable, he had – no, has – much influence. See how Adolf Hitler loves his music-dramas, and specially those based on German myth.'

'Oh, I know, don't think I don't understand. Please don't. It – it's like original sin, loving the work in spite of – It's such potent stuff, goes right deep under the skin. Think of Lohengrin's farewell. And the *Parsifal* Good Friday music. It either hits you in the midriff or it doesn't – isn't that why he's either loved or hated?'

'Wagner is the old sorcerer, Klingsor himself,' agreed Franz. His frown cleared, he seemed amused by my fervour.

'You don't sound exactly immune yourself.'

'I am not. Only – Bayreuth! One of the Nazis' holy places.'

'Is it as bad as that? I didn't know. I'm ignorant, really. Perhaps I shouldn't go, anyway. My father was dead against my travelling in Germany. He didn't even want me to come here, either.'

'He was right about Germany. Perhaps about here, too. Perhaps we should not even go to the mountains alone, Nell. You saw why, last night.' His mouth was grim. It made him look much older.

'Is it always like this now? Everything so welcoming on the surface, but underneath – ' At home people were always worrying about Hitler and possible war; at least he wasn't just the other side of some mountains.

Franz said heavily, 'Day by day it grows worse.'

I tried to think of something comforting to say. It was impossible. Anyway, just then Tommy began marshalling the choir together.

'You are singing second, we are fifth,' said Franz. 'And I watch you from in front, Nell. There is not room for more than two choir in the artists' room.'

'Don't beat us, will you?'

'Of course. In the end.'

'Oh, in the end!'

We separated, laughing, and I went to join the others. Cassie was pale green. 'Cheer up, we can only muck it, or be sick,' I told her. She turned emerald, and Tommy shot me a glance sharp as a Valkyrie's spear.

Poor Cassie, I thought loftily, from my superior experience. Then nemesis struck and as we filed on to the dais I felt pea-green as our youngest member. For long minutes we stood staring into the brightly-lit Hall, with all those critical faces staring back at us, undimmed by darkness.

Then:

> Have you seen but a bright lily grow,
> Before rude hands have touched it,
> Have you marked but the fall of the snow –

How I loved to sing, it gave me a wonderful charged sense of freedom. A seagull riding the waves. Something fragile yet paradoxically tough, in touch with the elements. And always it was a way into something larger, more expansive, than oneself.

'O so white, O so soft, O so sweet is she.' Gina dug me meaningly in the ribs with her elbow.

I could hardly judge our performance. There was quite good applause, anyway. We had finished gently, with a twilight silveriness of tone till the sound swelled, and died. We waited till the clapping stopped, then Tommy raised her hand again, and with a little nod released us into our second offering, Brahms's 'How lovely are thy dwellings'. There was greater applause this time, before we filed out demurely ('Like thoroughly nice English girls,' whispered Gina, causing me to choke).

Seated in the auditorium I barely noticed the other choirs until Franz sang again. I was only really alive now in his presence. Unconsciously I was clasping Gina's arm in a painful grip.

'Relax, Nell. He's still there and – look! singing.'

Somebody hushed her.

I settle back to listen, though more concerned with watching Franz than with the subtleties of Bach or Mendelssohn. When his choir had taken their bow, and while we waited for the next, Gina murmured, 'Pull up, Nell. You're starting to act all humble. Talk about O so soft, I really tremble for you. In a year or two you'd be looking like that fat little Irma.'

'Can't help it.'

'Yes, you can. Try, anyway. And here they come.'

Their place was close to ours, and Franz managed to slip into the empty seat behind me.

'Nell. I have our concert tickets, from the foyer.'

'Oh, great. I didn't know we got them here.'

'Now we sit together.' He handed me my ticket.

'Wonderful, Franz.'

Again Gina's elbow in my ribs. 'Sweet spaniel,' she meant, but I was past caring.

'Did you like our programme?'

'Lovely. Even Tommy said it was.'

'The concert also will be good. This young girl who plays the Sibelius violin concerto is terrific, worth hearing. And today it would be bad day for the mountains, they wear their mist cap, the rain falls. It may be better tomorrow.'

Gina pinched my arm. 'Tommy drew all our tickets on the way in,' she hissed. I gazed at her blankly, and she shook her head in despair, rolling her eyes in good imitation of lunacy.

At lunchtime Tommy was surprisingly mellow: 'Girls, we held our own.' I seized the chance to tell her that I was double-booked for the concert.

'Never mind, dear, we'll return a ticket to the box office when we go in. Let me see yours, oh – that's further back, I should hand it in; someone else will need it.'

'Well, er – actually – Franz got them for us both, Miss Armstrong.'

Her glance was darkly sardonic. She sniffed. 'Herr Schmidt speaks quite well of that young man. This time I will hand in a ticket. In future check with me first, Eleanor.'

'Thank you, Miss Armstrong.' I felt myself redden as all down our long table beady eyes were fixed knowingly on me. Grins and nudgings and giggles. Little beasts.

Sitting with an empty seat beside me I waited tensely for Franz, afraid he might have been attacked again. This terror was going to be an integral part of our love; I must accept that and learn to live with it. When he came at last, frowning and alone, my pulses stuttered back to normal.

His greeting was abrupt, almost cool. 'I was – detain, Nell. My family – my father, I mean.'

'Is he ill?'

'No, not that. Nell, would it displease you if we miss the mountains tomorrow? We could picnic along the valley of the Inn instead, then perhaps you would come back for tea and meet him.'

I tried to smother my disappointment. And suppose his father didn't like me? Anyone who has ever loved must dread that moment of intrusion by the solid presences of parents, friends, a whole undiscovered background.

'All right. Anyway, we won't need to take anyone with us on that sort of drive, will we? Not if we've got a car?'

'No, we need not. I have my own car, and I am fast driver, but very safe.'

Fat little Irma with the lovely voice was sitting by us, accompanied by a stalwart young German who had done equally well in the solos. Now she turned to me with an ingratiating smile and began talking across him in a hotch-potch of German-English.

'Sie sind Engländerin, nicht wahr – Mees Dobell? Whoo – ' like an owl – 'singing in solo contest are? Both, then, we go together into – the – the – '

'Quarter-final,' I helped her out.

She wriggled and beamed like a fat puppy. 'Remember, Heinrich? – Mees Dobell *singt wie eine Nachtigall.'*

I pinched Franz's arm, and he came to my rescue; luckily, since Irma was a compulsive chatterer. Her companion put a word in now and then, but she was soon off again, talking over both our heads to Franz. I was thankful when the concert began at last with the overture to *The Magic Flute*. To this day I can never hear those solemn opening chords without their bringing back the touch of Franz's hand on mine, the warmth of his presence in that uncertain world and time.

I leaned dreamily against his shoulder and gave myself up to enchantment.

In spite of our obvious reluctance Irma, Heinrich in tow, attached herself to us during the interval. Small she might be, but she was a miniature tank. On her command the boys were dispatched to fetch refreshment while she whisked me to a corner table, plumping herself down just in time to thwart another party.

'*Reserviert*,' she pronounced, dropping her bag on to the empty seat beside her, and indicating I should do the same. Having settled things to her liking, she demanded to know what I thought of Austria?

In my halting German I replied that I loved everything here: people, mountains, music, and above all the famous Austrian charm.

Ah! Then I would love Germany more. Everything that was good in Austria was better still in Germany. What, I had never been there? But what a chance for me if I could win tickets for Bayreuth! '*Hör zu*, El-ean-or – ' and she went gabbling on about what a fabulous chance it would be for me to see Germany's renaissance at first hand, and how I could then explain to my family and friends what lies were told about the poor German people whose State was a State to be proud of, with the best Leader in the world, the beloved Führer.

When I could interrupt her I murmured that I'd always thought the beloved Führer was Austrian?

Something behind those friendly eyes looked out coldly for a moment, then she smiled, patting my hand with her small plump palm. Yes, of course, I was quite right, and it showed the Führer's greatness that he had chosen to work and live in Germany, while desiring that Austria should be part of the magnificent Third Reich. '*Denken Sie nur*, El-eanor – if you should ticket have for Bayreuth, you might the Führer see!'

I knew that Hitler was a great lover of Richard Wagner's music, and was often at the *Festspielhaus*, the famous opera house that had been specially built to house festivals of Wagner's works. When Irma suggested that I might actually see him there one part of me felt a sneaking, shameful desire to view her Führer in the flesh, something no one I knew had ever done. Who can deny the fascination of monsters? All the same I was disgusted by her spaniel-like devotion.

'I don't suppose I'll win,' I said. 'Here come Franz and Heinrich.'

They were fighting their way back to us bearing steins of beer for themselves and ices for Irma and me. Beside me she was chattering on, ' – *natürlich*, Bruno Walter will never Conductor at Bayreuth be again, *weil er Jude* – Jew – *ist* – ' She broke off, looking from me to Franz. 'Walter,' she repeated thoughtfully, fixing her beady little eyes on his face.

I stood up, retrieving my bag. 'We must go, Irma. I'm afraid Miss Armstrong – my music teacher – will be expecting us to join her, won't she, Franz?' Leaving her openmouthed, I seized Franz by the arm and guided him across the room to a table behind a pillar, well hidden from her prying eyes as well as Tommy's sarcastic ones.

'My rescuer,' said Franz, amused. 'But why so sudden, Nell?'

'They were *echt Deutsch*, all right,' I said evasively 'and I rather think they are *echt* Nazi too. Irma did nothing but extol the Führer. I'm not sure I would go to Bayreuth after all, even if I won some tickets.'

7

Time, since Franz and I first met, had developed for me an awkward habit of sometimes stretching itself out, sometimes telescoping; so today I lost the middle of the 'Jupiter' Symphony entirely. Under cover of clapping I murmured, 'There's a Reception tonight, isn't there? Gina says the alternative's some awful film on Beethoven.'

'So? I shall not be at either.'

Franz's tone was cool, indifferent. These sudden changes! The same rigidity as on that earlier occasion, the same sudden cut-off.

'Why, though? Tell me.'

'Not now. Not here.'

'Franz, something's the matter? Let me help.'

'There is no way you can help.' His voice was bleak. 'After this concert I must to home. So – ' He touched my hand, briefly. 'Now it is "*wiedersehen*". Tomorrow I will fetch you from your *Gasthof, ja*?' Before I could speak he had slipped from his seat and was shouldering his way out of the room. High-handed, I thought it. Didn't he love and trust me, after all? I still knew him so little. Perhaps this was how he always treated girls. Suddenly I was very much aware of being a foreigner among people whose language was hard for me; worse, whose charming surfaces hid sinister pitfalls.

'Hi,' said Tim's voice behind me. 'Abandoned you, has he? Not much of a stayer, your *Rosenkavalier*.'

'He had to get home,' I snapped. 'Something wrong. Where's Gina – and Dan?'

'Old Guard actually in favour again?'

'Wasn't the violinist great?' Gina and Dan materialized on my other side. 'Where's Black Beauty?'

'You may well ask, G. *Küss die Hand* has gone to graze elsewhere; so we, my poppet, are to support the abandoned one, though personally I'm – '

' – blocking the gangway.' I turned my shoulder on them and began forcing my way out towards the foyer.

Gina's hand was on my arm. 'Don't be so touchy, Nell. Listen, we've a plan for tonight, not for Tommy's ears.'

'What sort of plan?' I said dully.

'Don't sound so excited! Tommy and Ruddigore are off to that Reception and signed up most of us, but Dan and Tim and I are opting out. You too, I imagine. So we've got tickets for that awful film, and one for you, super alibis because – '

'Look out, here's Tommy,' warned Dan. 'Wait till we're outside.'

'Just watch me take on Tommy,' said Gina. 'Nell must lie low, she's not wholly Lost in Music. Hullo, Miss Armstrong! Wasn't the "Jupiter" absolutely – well, *absolutely*?'

'A judgement I should expect from a junior, Regina. I thought some of the dynamics ill-chosen, the tempo of the second movement questionable. And I must speak about your rude behaviour, you positively trampled over the *Fürstin* – the Princess – at the row's end.'

'I'm sorry. Honestly didn't know I trod on some highborn toes. Shall I nip back to apologize?'

'I did so for you, she is a very charming woman. You may speak to her yourself at the Reception, she chairs the committee, and has much to do with sponsoring this Contest.'

'Ah, well . . . We meant to ask if we might go to the film instead, people rave about it.'

'And who are "we"? Has this to do with that young man of Eleanor's?'

'Franz Walter has gone home and won't be back today,' I said hastily. 'It's just the four of us.'

A frosty look from Tommy, whose intuition had uncanny little antennae, almost visible. 'They say it is an educational film, I should have liked to see it myself.'

'Oh, you mustn't miss the Reception, *noblesse oblige* and all that,' said Dan. 'And Ruddi- Mr. Scroggworthy is only going because you'll be there. His German's not so hot, you know.'

'I would not care to let down a colleague. Nor the dear Princess. But you boys must behave, and look after the girls.'

'Sure we will. Handcuff them to our sides.'

'And I believe Cassie might go with you, I'll just mention it.' Tommy wore her 'trumped you' expression. I saw Gina open her mouth to protest, and said quickly, 'Yes, do ask Cassie, please.'

'Why not beg her to come herself?' hissed Gina as we walked sedately back to the *Gasthof*. 'You clown, Nell. Cassie! That's put paid to Peter's plan.'

'We can put Cassie off, somehow. Tommy only pushed her at you because we're such an untrustworthy lot. Anyway, what is Peter's plan?' I said rather gloomily. Still, whatever it was, it might take my thoughts off Franz's cavalier cut-off.

'His friend Ludwig's got a car, and there's some special eating place they know of, up in the mountains. Think of it, by moonlight. What's the matter – you don't sound keen. Don't you want to come?'

'Tommy's on the look-out for Bad Behaviour.'

'Oh Nell, don't be so damping. What's come over you, since Black Beauty?'

'Don't call him that. Why can't you all leave me alone about him?' Just then I was almost wishing we'd never come here, that I'd never set eyes on Franz. Gina put an arm around my shoulders. 'Nell? I'm sorry, we were only teasing. Something wrong?'

'Yes, I think so, though he wouldn't let me in on it. Perhaps he's just gone off me.' I pulled out my handkerchief and scrubbed at my eyes. 'Walk on, for cripes' sake.'

'We don't have to go, if you don't want to.'

'No, I do, I do really, but – I've just got an awful doomish feeling about everything; black, in all directions. And we can't risk getting locked out of the *Gasthof*.'

'I'll talk to Anna. She's there till midnight. She's not much older than us, look how she helped you before. Ah, come on, Nell! Now how do we sidetrack Cassie?'

We were up in our own room, changing, when we heard Cassie's knock. Gina dashed over to the washstand, seized a tumbler of bright blue liquid, and began to gargle. I opened the door. 'Come along in, Cass, we're not quite ready. Tommy left for the Reception yet?'

'She's downstairs.' Cassie spoke absently, her eyes were fixed on Gina. 'Is Gina ill?'

'We *hope* not. I made her get that stuff at the chemist's, as insurance. She gets bad throats so easily.'

Cassie was known to guard her own voice and health as though she were the Queen of Song.

'We can muffle her up well,' I said encouragingly, 'and she can sit between you and me so she won't have to talk.'

'Well truly, I – I just looked in to say I'd changed my mind about the Reception, it will be more fun, you see. Do make sure Gina does nothing rash – think of the Choir. Shall I tell Tommy?'

'Heavens, no. Don't spoil her evening. Hurry, Cass, you'll be late.'

The door slammed, and footfalls could be heard hurrying towards the stairs. Gina was spluttering blue bubbles through her laughter. 'Oh, Nell, Nell! You've sheer genius.'

'Morally indefensible, Regina,' I said in Tommy's best manner. Neither of us could stop laughing, till a second tapping on the door announced the arrival of Anna, carrying a bundle of garments.

'I bring you the dresses Fraülein Gina ask about.' She began tenderly laying out two sets of Austrian national costume on my bed. 'They belong to my greatest friend, they please you, yes?' She smoothed the laces of a velvet bodice. 'She lend them with much pleasure. I am not the same shape as the Fräuleins, no?'

'*Dear* Anna.' Gina hugged her. 'You're an apple dumpling. And that's very nice.'

Anna looked puzzled, though pleased by our delight.

'You will not back home too late come? And where do you go? This I will know, please.'

'The place is called *Zum Goldner Adler*, in the mountains.'

'With two boys, *nicht wahr*? And does the old Fräulein who look always *so* – ' Anna drew down the corners of her mouth – 'know this, and approve?'

'She knows about the boys,' temporized Gina. She held up one of the dresses against herself, and looked approvingly in the glass.

'But she thought we were going to a film,' I added. Anna must know; it would be a shame to get her into hot water. 'It's really three boys and a friend with a car.'

'And this friend, how old is she?' Anna was stroking the other dress lovingly as though she might change her mind about leaving it. I held out my arms, and she surrendered it reluctantly.

'Older, since he has this car,' I murmured, struggling into the dress.

'Four boys! You lose me my place.' Poor Anna looked rather scared. She took the laces from me and pulled them so tight that I felt like a breathless Victorian Miss. 'You promise, to return not late?'

'Absolutely.' Gina twirled round so that the dress swirled about her like poppy petals. 'There! And you look smashing, Nell. That blue's your colour. I look so frumpish with these plaits, beside your pageboy.'

'It would be shame to cut them, Fräulein. Look – ' Anna pulled her round to face herself in the glass, and deftly twined her plaits into a heavy coronal. 'Now I pin – like this – *So!*'

'It certainly suits you,' I said, almost jealous of Gina's sudden glamour. 'There'll be no holding Peter.'

Gina was regarding herself with an expression of ingenuous amazement. 'Nell, we'll have a gorgeous time. Even without your Franz.'

We waited for our escorts at the rear of the *Gasthof*, in its former stable courtyard. The evening sky had the luminous sheen of pearl, and the air was warm with summer. In the courtyard corner the branches of a giant lime rose almost to rooftop level. Light from the windows eerily lit the topmost leaves, turning them to acid green as they moved to and fro, fanned by drifting currents of air. More light was reflected upward from silver-grey cobbles. It was like being submerged at the bottom of a warm pool.

We waited. There was a sense of strangeness and expectation. No car, no sound but our quick nervous breathing. I began to hope they wouldn't come, then we could go tamely back inside and join the juniors at boring supper. It wasn't just that I was missing Franz. In these moments of waiting I had sensed something like unpierceable mist coiled ahead of me in the future, more mysterious and menacing than Siegfried's dragon, chilling as ice.

'Nell? You look goose-green – or is it the light? You okay? Here they are, at last.'

The car swept into the courtyard and halted with a screech of brakes.

'Arriving with a flourish,' I said sourly.

'Don't you really want to come?'

'No,' I muttered, weakly allowing myself to be pulled on to the back seat by Dan and Tim. Gina was climbing into the front, between Peter and Ludwig.

'Do keep her off the gears,' begged Tim.

Peter merely laughed. The headlights described a circle of gold as the car headed for the road, just missing oncoming traffic. I longed to cry: Stop, let me go back! Afraid of mockery – self-mockery too – I was dumb. Tim's arm was round my waist, Dan's round my shoulders. There was a yell from Gina as Ludwig manipulated her ankle instead of the gears.

'All together now, drown the squawking: "We'll be coming round the mountain"' sang Dan, boomingly.

> We'll be coming round the mountain,
> Coming round the mountain (sing up, girls!)
> Coming round the mountain –

The car sped on, just avoiding a coach. Soon Peter, and even Ludwig, were joining in:

> Kommin' round the mountain when we kom.

By the time we reached the village, lights were shining out one by one in Innsbruck far below, matching those in the darkening sky above. I followed Tim from the car. He looked about him appreciatively. 'This is *something*. Come on, Nell.' Taking my hand he dragged me towards a low wall overlooking the drop beneath, where the land sloped precipitously to the valley. Up here a stiff breeze bounced off the high peaks and buffeted our faces as we gazed down on the windings of the Inn. Glowworm trails of villages marked its course. Here and there on farther mountain peaks sparks of light beamed out from isolated châlets.

'What a place. You know, I almost envy these people. Some Golden Eagle's nest! The simple life, the mountains all around you and Innsbruck below when you're bored; Salzburg at the end of the line. The simple life,' Tim repeated emphatically.

'I shouldn't think it's all that simple but real hard work. And they probably spend half their lives in mist.'

Leaning on the wall, I propped my chin on my hands. Where was Franz now? Even in thought I couldn't follow him since he hadn't told me exactly where he lived. He might be home with his father, somewhere on the outskirts of the town itself, or – For the first time my imagination dreamed up another girl: someone always known to him, someone his father expected him to marry. My eyes searched the darkening landscape as though I could force it to reveal his presence in one of those glowworm villages . . .

'Tim, look.' I grabbed his arm.

'Look at what – where?'

I pointed excitedly. 'Over there. A – a sort of flare, or – is it a fire, up there among that dark mass of firs? On that mountain flank, don't you *see*?'

'What if it is? Don't get so excited, you're all of a twitch these days, Nell. It's just some sort of torchlight procession forming, I'd say.'

'Among those trees?' I said disbelievingly.

'They're dwarfed from here, there may be open ground. Wonder what's happening, exactly?' His voice betrayed a flicker of interest. 'It is a procession of some sort, a fire would move upward with this breeze – that's going straight across.'

'It's not a procession. See? The tail's still where it was. The front's changing course, though.'

We watched. Someone – or several people – was drawing in flame on the mountainside.

'Lines of bonfires ready set? Brushwood, probably,' mused Tim.

A minute or two passed till the design flamed up complete. A swastika, burning fiercely in the night air, branding the earth; a mark of ownership flaring brutally above the placid countryside.

'Oh, God,' I said, shivering.

'Cold, Nell? Come inside.' Tim's voice was unusually gentle. 'Don't suppose we'll find any of these damned Nazis up here.'

8

Peter's friend Ludwig had booked seats at one end of the long table at the centre of the tiny dining room. Savoury smells drifted in through the half-open door beyond a well-stocked bar. The restaurant was still almost empty, its only other customers – a boy in Tyrolean costume with his girl – were tucked romantically away in the far corner.

When Tim took in the full splendour of our borrowed finery he let out a shrill whistle.

'No vulgar comments, please,' said Gina, settling herself at the table.

When I turned my head and glanced through the window behind me that arrogantly flaming Nazi symbol was still there. My awareness of it made me also aware that the waitress who brought our Moselle was scared: she barely paused to offer us the menu before retreating behind the bar to talk in agitated whispers with the innkeeper, whose expression was equally grave. The challenge of that fiery crooked cross imprinted itself on my mind's eye.

'Drink up, Nell,' urged Tim. 'Going to sit in this sort of trance all through dinner? Never seen one of old Adolf's swastikas before?'

'Not – not like that.' I shuddered. 'So – so aggressive. These people – the landlord and the girl – are hating it too, can't you see?'

'It's their country not ours, thank God.'

'Don't be heartless.'

'And don't tease the girl,' put in Dan. 'Lend her your

hankie to wipe dem big eyes – don't you see, it's Count Drac's country? That's the crux of it.'

'And Peter's too,' said Gina. '*Und Peter ist* so – over-*ge kommt*, bistn't *du, Peter?*'

At that, both Peter and Ludwig collapsed into laughter, restraint lifted, and I felt more able to tackle the menu, even though my thoughts were with Franz, and what that evil sign could mean to him. I was dreading that it might have something to do with his secretive departure.

'This soup's an entire meal in itself,' Gina was wailing. 'How will we sing anything tomorrow, Nell?'

'"I lay on my tum and tried to hum, but only a rumbling seemed to come"' misquoted Tim.

Ludwig looked at them hopelessly.

'This lack of Esperanto or whatever does slow things up, doesn't it? Wine, wine and more wine, that's the only answer.' Tim imperiously beckoned the waitress. 'Gina, you make an effort. Why are you just lolling there giggling, with Peter's arm round you?'

'*I* am not shy. I know English, some,' pronounced Ludwig suddenly. 'You will see. And I think. This is all.'

'Splendid,' said Tim. 'Share the conclusions.'

'I think you not understanding are how it now with us is. Two country, so near with same language. What is wrong they together march?'

'March? Are you a Nazi?' I glanced at Peter, who didn't meet my eyes. Or perhaps he was just fully occupied with Gina's.

Ludwig made a sweeping movement of his hand. 'The culture. The roots, yes, alike . . . beside, why should it that I, Ludwig – ' he struck himself on the chest – 'should split be? When my mother from Germany is?'

'You're free to go to and fro across the frontier, aren't you?'

'There should no frontier,' said Ludwig. 'There must be – '

'"*Ein Volk, ein Reich, ein Führer*?" Could you really stomach him, the shouting, strutting, lying – and you an Austrian?'

Ludwig glowered at me. Peter might have warned us about him, I thought. If he's not an active party member he's the next best thing.

'Nell, no politics tonight,' said Tim wisely. 'Pleasure, that's what we're here for.' He refilled our glasses. 'Here's to the immortal soul of Franz Schubert, coupled with the doubly immortal one of Wolfgang Mozart.' He raised his glass and drank deeply.

Gina swung hers in semicircles, squinting at it. Wine drops flew.

'You're tipsy, eat something, my girl, for heaven's sake. Here come our *Schnitzels. Danke schön, mein schönes Mädchen,'* said Tim in a lofty way. If Ludwig was going to drive us home I hoped he had a stronger head.

By this time the room was filling up. There was talk and laughter. Even the waitress was smiling, and someone had pinned a spray of jasmine to the velvet bodice of her dress.

'Gemütlich, so so *gemütlich* here,' murmured Gina. She looked altogether too *gemütlich,* her coils of hair slipping sideways, her blouse off one shoulder. And Ludwig had begun putting wine away at an amazing rate.

'Tim – Dan! Do stop them drinking so much.'

'Whatsa matter with you, Nell? Mustn't fuss, s'boring,' Tim reproved me. 'Tum-tum-ti-*tum*-tum,' and he started tapping out what he imagined was the rhythm of a waltz.

I had an eerie sense of being split. On one hand, Tim's banal tune, and those dedicated beerswillers close by, loud and cheerful. While outside, beyond the inn, lay those lonely mountains, and valleys concealing sinister crimes and miseries summed up by a flaming swastika.

I held out my glass for Ludwig to refill.

'Thash ticket, Nell, thash more like it,' said Dan, while Tim clasped his head in both hands, and began humming 'the Blue Danube'. The humming grew and swelled till I realized it wasn't just Tim's, but the engine hum of some large car labouring up the road to the inn.

Every head in the room turned to watch the arrival of a large shiny Mercedes filled to overflowing with a bunch of toughs. A rakish two-seater followed, driven by a uniformed officer. Both cars drew up in the circle of light outside the door. The newcomers were noisily full of horseplay. With the exception of the officer one and all of them were brownshirts.

I saw the landlord stiffen.

'Guten Abend, Herr Mejor Graf.'

So that's Herr Graf, I thought, critically eyeing the newcomer. Not so badlooking either, if he weren't wearing some constipated type of uniform and shiny jackboots. Jackboots, over the Austrian border. Maybe the Austrian Nazis went in for them too; anyway – Austrian or German – what was he doing in the company of these louts?

Suddenly I found him staring back at me, and felt myself blushing. I looked away.

Hurried arrangements were being made to seat the party. Some tables were shoved together against the bar. The brownshirts pushed past us with unnecessary vigour, calling noisily for beer, while the officer still hovered in the doorway, chatting with the landlord – in German, of course, although it was simple enough for me to understand: 'My good Bauer, they won't care where their table is so long as they can drink – but I'm delighted to see you're entertaining a young relative of mine, so bring a chair for me to join him.'

'Korbinion – Korbi!' Ludwig half rose, flapping his napkin in drunken greeting.

Gina didn't appear to notice. She was practically lying in Peter's arms. I sat up very straight, thanking heaven for Franz's absence.

'Nell, my lovely, who'sh this Tales-from-Vienna-Woodsh type?' Tim waved his glass wildly till a stream of wine shot across the table. *'Grüss Gott,'* he said thickly, bowing to no one in particular.

Ludwig shifted his chair sideways, so that Bauer could place a chair between us.

'Ludwig, I'd no idea you arranged such charming little suppers here,' said the Graf. His gaze roved over Gina, with contempt, I thought, then he settled himself at my side, putting a negligent arm around my waist.

Furious, I struggled free. The wretched man could hardly be blamed for his mistake, though, considering what Gina looked like.

'Owl! *Dummkopf!*' I hissed at Ludwig, 'Sort your relative out, can't you?'

He may not have understood my words, but he understood the tone all right, and poured a flood of apologetic German into his cousin's ears.

The Graf, however, merely looked more amused.

'I have made a mistake? Forgive me, Fräulein.'

'Yes, a big mistake, Herr Graf,' I replied primly, feeling ridiculous as Ludwig floundered through introductions, ending with some pompous phrase about our being music students representing our country at the Innsbruck contests. A subtle change came over the Graf's expression; amusement was tempered by respect. At least they do all genuinely love music, I thought.

'Fraülein, believe me, I was misled by appearances.' A flicker of a glance at Gina.

There was nothing I could say to that. I changed the subject: 'You speak better English than Ludwig. It's a relief. I'm not too good at German, Herr Graf.'

'I was at Oxford for two years. Please let us be finished with "Herr Graf". Call me Korbinion, better still, Korbi – after all, you are with my young cousin.'

'I'll call you Graf Korbinion', I said firmly.

He laughed. 'You are very correct, Fraülein.' Another amused glance at Gina.

'Gina – sit *up*,' I hissed across the table. 'My friend is totally unused to wine,' I told him.

'Obviously. She will be very sick if she drinks more.' Graf Korbinion beckoned to the landlord, and gave him an order.

The man soon returned with a carafe, which he set down at Gina's elbow. 'Let her drink plenty of that,' said the Graf, 'and she will soon recover. It is our friend Bauer's speciality: potent, and non-alcoholic.'

I was immensely relieved, and grateful. If Tommy saw Gina now! When I had expressed my thanks I said, awkwardly changing the subject, 'Your name, Korbinion, is unusual, isn't it?'

He shrugged. 'It is in my family. My full name is Wilhelm Maximilian – Rudolph – Ottobeuren – Dietrich – von und zu but one of my godmothers was so devout! – Dietrich von und zu Westerhausern.'

I ticked it off slowly on my fingers: 'Korbinion – Wilhelm – Maximilian – Rudolph – Ottbeuren – Dietrich – von und zu Westerhausern.'

'Excellent! Well done.'

'Why the von *und* zu? Must you be from and to?'

'Ah,' he said lightly, 'it is because my family has been clever enough to hold to its original estates in Germany. 'Zu' means we are still there.'

'So you are German, then? I thought so.'

'Certainly. Do you not approve?'

I didn't answer that, outright. 'Ludwig is your cousin. At least neither of you is named Adolf.'

'My family served always in the Imperial Army. My father won the Iron Cross on the Somme. This uniform is of my father's regiment, I too am Uhlan; and I do not wear the brown shirt, as you see.'

To be anti-Hitler in Germany must be difficult. I was sorry if I had offended him, after his easy kindness to Gina.

Just then loud laughter reached a crescendo at the brownshirts' table. Graf Korbinion turned his head and spoke one cutting sentence. Abruptly the laughter died. If he were anti-Hitler what was he doing in command of them, as it seemed? Specially this side of the border.

'Those toughs are Austrian, aren't they? Don't you keep

rather odd company, for an Uhlan?'

'I come here often,' he said shortly. 'I have relatives here, like Ludwig for example. It was – known – there would be demonstrations of some kind tonight. And – see how I trust you, Fräulein – I was invited over to make sure nothing got – out of hand, you would say.'

'You mean, the fire? That swastika?'

'Ah, you saw it, then?'

'We could hardly help it. Tim – my friend – and I were leaning on that parapet, looking at the view – the mountains; then – that sign, flaring.' My thoughts flew to Franz. I added huskily, 'I hope there wasn't – I mean, no actual fighting, nobody was hurt?'

'A few heads broken. Fräulein Nell, you look upset? Young men do fight, you know. They enjoy it. This was nothing very serious, anyway. My presence restrained them.'

'You said you were "invited over". That means the local authorities knew all about it first? The Germans too?'

'Oh, yes. After all, big brother Germany is just across the border. Many Austrian officials are heartily in favour of us, and find signs of popular support welcome, so long as they are not too violent and antagonize people.'

'All Austrians aren't in favour of an *Anschluss*,' I said hotly.

'No, indeed. And especially not Jews. But, my well-informed Fräulein Nell, politics are dull stuff, after all. Let us talk of something else. You interest me. The way your hand clutches your glass when I speak of broken heads!'

He was too observant, and he had the manner of someone whose ancestors were used to the habit of command. I wasn't surprised that he had been asked to watchdog a demonstration; or would 'orchestrate it' be nearer the truth?

'I l-love Austria,' I stammered, regretting I had shown my feelings. 'I've always loved it.'

'You have been here so often?'

'Three or four times.'

'How charming then, that you care so much what happens

here. These, after all, are not your problems.'

'You said we'd talk of something else.'

'Agreed. Let us speak of music instead, it is my passion.'

I glanced at Tim to see how he was taking this, but he was staring fixedly into his glass. Neither he nor Dan would have said more to a stranger than that music was okay, not bad stuff, something to pass the time.

'You are here with a choir, Ludwig says.'

'I am a soloist too.'

'Wonderful! What is your voice? Mezzo? Then they will always try to force it higher. Do not let them, Fräulein Nell, a "made" voice is always terrible. May we now drop the "Fräulein"?'

'All right,' I said, ungraciously.

'Good, also this terrible "Graf Korbinion", which make me feel one hundred years old? Now tell me of this festival, this contest. *Natürlich*, I hear of it, since my aunt is Patroness.'

'Your aunt is the *Fürstin*, then?' I was impressed in spite of myself. 'Well, so far we've had the elimination heats for all the entrants in our different groups, so it's just the quarter-, semi-finals and finals to come.'

'*So*! Both Nell and choir through to quarter-finals. And when is soloists' day?'

'The day after tomorrow. Tomorrow it's strings and woodwind.'

'Excellent, you have a free day. Perhaps I could show you something of the countryside, places you have not seen?'

'How kind, but tomorrow I can't,' I said, thinking – and hoping – that I sounded like my mother in one of her freeze-you-out moods.

'*Schade*. Perhaps I will take leave and come to hear the quarter-final instead. What do you sing?'

Just then Tim, who had seemed to be paying no attention to anything around him, said thickly, 'Poor old Drac. Odds on Tales from Vi'nna Woodsh.' And Gina, who had been swilling Bauer's special mixture, roused herself to say,

'Shouldn't have cut your hair, Nell,' to which Dan added, 'Our little Lorelei.'

I frowned at them ferociously. This Ruritanian Count's interest was quite heady stuff, and I might have enjoyed it if it weren't for Franz. Now it was a dreadful undesired complication. I looked at my watch, and gave a startled yelp.

'Gina, the time! We should be going.'

Korbinion looked far from flattered. 'Going? Surely not yet, Ludwig's car is here outside.'

'No, we must go; we're not really officially here.'

'Aha, I see. Truanting, yes?'

'Yes. Our alibi's some awful film on Beethoven. Come on, G.'

'Peter says it won't take more than twenty minutes downhill,' she protested.

'But there's always punctures – '

'Ludwig will see you safely home, he is reliable, like me. Now tell me, have you ever been to Germany?'

'No, never. Gina – '

'Again, *Schade*. Then you have never been to hear a Wagner opera at Bayreuth, this should be remedied. This year they give performances of *Parsifal*, also of course the four operas of *Der Ring des Nibelungen* – you know them, naturally? "The Rhinegold", "The Valkyrie", "Siegfried" and "Twilight of the Gods" – *Götterdämmerung*. Will you give me the pleasure to be my guest? My aunt always takes a villa for Bayreuth, she would be delighted for you to stay. All very correct, believe me. If you wish, she would write to your parents.'

'*Cripes*,' said Gina.

I felt myself go scarlet. 'But I – I don't think . . . in fact, I'm almost sure, I won't be able to, I mean – Herr Graf, I – '

'Korbi.'

'Yes, but – ' I scowled at Gina, who was openly giggling.

'What a chance, don't be so wet, Nell,' Tim intervened drunkenly. 'You'd jump at it if it weren't for old Dr- ' Under my quelling glare he subsided.

'Old Dr– ?'

'Our old dragon of a music teacher,' I said desperately.

'You will introduce me, certainly. I will persuade her.'

'It's just – I might be going there already – it depends on – on who wins – there are some seats for successful soloists, and – '

'Splendid. You will be popular if you win them and give them away.'

I've never much cared for what's called the habit of command; his hectoring attitude restored my sang-froid.

'Now I understand why you were asked to cope single-handed with that demonstration.'

He looked flattered. Probably he put my reaction down to gaucheness and maidenly confusion.

'You would wish to come, surely? I shall speak to my aunt.'

'Bayreuth would be lovely, if it weren't that there are such complications – ' I looked desperately at Gina. 'G. We must be going – do remember Anna.'

She stumbled to her feet. Unfortunately the bunch from the Mercedes had downed quantities of beer and were leaving too. There was heavy bumping into chairs and cursing, subdued as they passed our table. Graf Korbinion watched them go with a critical eye. The last man staggered, and was supported to the car. Its engine was violently revved.

I was just saying, 'There goes your responsibility,' when there was an echoing series of bangs, followed by a slithering sound and nasty final crash.

Korbinion reached the door a short head before the inn-keeper. Our party wasn't far behind. The Mercedes was being drunkenly reversed, and where Ludwig's car had stood by the lowest sweep of parapet there was nothing; the wall itself was a scatter of crumbled stones.

Ludwig let out a cry which echoed lingeringly in my heart. Korbinion was volubly cursing the brownshirts. I plucked at his arm and shook it. 'Listen! Please listen – it's desperate. Never mind the car, if Gina and I aren't back within half an hour we'll be sent home to England.'

'That is desperate indeed. *So*! We must arrange.' He went aside to confer with Bauer, then returned to me, shaking his head. 'A car must come from Innsbruck. His own, unfortunately, is at the garage, his van in town.'

A low moan escaped me. He patted my arm. 'Courage. I myself will drive you back. At once.'

'Your car won't hold us all.'

'The Mercedes will.' He advanced on the band of brownshirts, now watching him with beaten-spaniel eyes.

''*raus*!'

He was hurriedly obeyed; but once the five of us, barely bothering to bid poor Ludwig goodnight, had piled into the limousine it would only reverse: the gears must have been damaged in the crash. We piled out again. My lips were trembling, and I gave a sob.

Korbinion was already opening the door of his two-seater must be my car after all, for you and Fraülein Gina. Your other friends must await the cab. Bauer will ring for one.'

'Whatever happens, don't you or Tim ever let on G. and I were up here with you,' I hissed at Dan. 'Understand?'

'Ratting on us?'

'This time, yes.'

Korbinion was already opening the door of his twoseater. 'It will be a squash, but – ' He helped Gina in, then held me back to murmur (and I could sense the amusement): 'One little moment. I have promised to see you safely home with no trouble, yes? One small condition, first. Bayreuth.'

'That's unfair. You made no conditions,' I said hotly.

He looked at his watch, and stood back.

I capitulated. 'All right, Herr Graf. If it's possible. But you – you deserve Hitler.'

He laughed; held some swift idiomatic exchange with Bauer about clearing the mess later, then got into the car after me, and we were off. He drove fast and well, in silence. I sensed both triumph and amusement, and had plenty of time to realize it might have been best to wait for the others. If Dan and Tim were in hot water with Ruddigore, Tommy was bound to guess we were involved. And now I had committed myself to future problems.

Once Gina said, 'It was mean, dropping the boys in the soup like that. I'll feel a pig if they're sent home and we're not.'

I was silent, biting my fingernails.

'You would too, if it wasn't for – '

'Oh, shut up, G.'

'For – ?' Korbinion cocked an interested ear.

'My solos,' I said firmly, and kicked Gina's ankle.

At our request, he set us down just short of the *Gasthof*. As we struggled from the car he said, 'I shall have the pleasure of seeing you on quarter-finals day. Goodnight, *Aschenputtel*.'

I said nothing whatever. As Gina and I scurried across the yard she muttered, '*Aschenputtel*? Sounds rude. What does he think we are?'

'It means Cinderella.'

'And he's ready to try on your glass slipper any day. What will Franz think?' She giggled.

'It's awful, it's no joke. You'll have to ride him off me.'

'Me? I wouldn't dare, a man who knows his own mind, I'd say. He just thought I was a drunk twit, anyway. Oh hello, Anna – here we are. Just in time.'

9

Next morning we scurried downstairs early, hoping to be through breakfast and out of range before Tommy could appear. 'We both look ghastly,' Gina said with truth, as we passed a long mirror in the hall.

I was just hissing at her, 'Can't you eat faster?' as I crammed a last bite of roll into my mouth, when Cassie arrived and Tommy's voice could be heard near the buttery crushing the waiter. Then she advanced on us.

'Good morning, girls. Regina, your hair! Have you no comb? A pity you two did not come to the Reception, the *Fürstin* specially asked after you, Eleanor; she takes a great interest in the soloists. A delightful evening, everyone so devoted to music. Cassie says Regina is developing a sore throat. I trust not, dear? You are somewhat pale. Are your glands all right?'

'Perfectly, thank you, Miss Armstrong.' Gina choked.

'Now, girls, I want to hear about the film. Worth missing the Reception, I hope.'

'We – er, didn't really think a lot of it,' muttered Gina.

'Strange, I was told it had wonderful reviews. Why did you not enjoy it, Eleanor?'

'Oh – one can hear the music on records, not so tinny. And he's not very like Beethoven, Rainer Mark, is he?'

'That dear, would be difficult. I have spoken to you before about arranging your thoughts in a more adult and interesting manner.'

'We didn't stay quite to the end, Miss Armstrong,' said Gina, taking our previously agreed line.

'Was the film really so poor?'

By this time the table was filling up with other choir members, ears pricked to hear Tommy grilling us.

'Or was it on account of Regina's throat?'

'Peter is so kind,' I said earnestly. 'Do you know, he borrowed his friend's car and took us all to a dear little place he knew where the landlord had just the right thing for her, didn't he, G.? She was soon feeling different, it was potent stuff.'

Gina choked again. 'Crumb,' she husked, avoiding Tommy's eye.

'Indeed. And at what hour did Peter-who-is-so-kind have the goodness to return you here?'

'Oh, before lock-up time, Miss Armstrong.' (One minute, in fact; I remembered Anna's relief, and our flight upstairs.)

'I am not at all happy about this. Who else went with you?'

'Dan and Tim, and Peter's friend Ludwig.'

There was a lengthy pause.

'Mr. Scroggworthy must look into this,' Tommy said at last. 'There will be more co-ordination in future. Eleanor, you are practising this morning, are you not? I have booked a studio for you from ten fifteen, they are next door to the Hall. You are on your honour to be conscientious, since I shall be supervising elsewhere. You can call for Dan on your way.'

'Yes, Miss Armstrong.' Beneath the table my hands clenched together in silent prayer. 'You – you gave me leave to go out with Franz Walter at twelve.'

A sniff. 'If I said so, I did. Where are you going?'

'He's bringing a picnic lunch so that we can eat it by the river. Then we're going to see his – his family. For tea.'

'Very well. Be back here by six-thirty. I do not want you tired out before your quarter-final.'

'Yes, Miss Armstrong. I mean, of course.'

'And see you behave yourself and keep – ' glacially –

'impromptu behaviour to a minimum. As for you, Regina, you are extremely pallid. We shall all sit out in the garden and look through our concert work together. Then I shall consult Mr. Scroggworthy about last night.'

I spent a miserable morning. Dan and Tim were furious with us for our cowardly exit, and it took a while before Dan could be cajoled into playing for me. At least I was glad to learn that they had managed to climb into their hotel room at one in the morning without discovery.

Practice over, though, my other worries returned. If only Franz and I hadn't parted yesterday on that sour note. Suppose he'd been mixed up with those rowdies last night, today he could be hurt, unable to meet me. And if we did meet, whatever would he say about Bayreuth with Korbinion? I parted from Dan, and rushed back to the *Gasthof*.

Gina was waiting for me. 'Tommy knows!'

'Oh Lord! How? And how much?' I slumped down on a chair.

'One of the *chers collègues* told her we shunned the Beethoven.'

'Good grief! Who – and why?'

'That Frenchwoman. Said she'd looked out for us all, specially you. Said it was a pity we all missed such an excellent film.'

'Horrible woman. She must have eyes like gimlets.'

'Nell, you're to stay in now. Tommy's reading the riot act before lunch, and holding an inquiry.'

'Where is she now?'

'Polishing the thumbscrews. Seriously, she's gone to rope in Ruddigore. We're all in the mulligatawny.'

'Look, you haven't seen me.'

'Idiot. She told me to wait up here for you.'

'I could have run into Franz in the street, couldn't I? That's what I'll do, now.'

'You'll only make things worse.'

'Could I? Listen, I've got to have today with him, you don't understand . . . . Poor Gina! I'm asking a lot, I know.'

'You are, rather. She'll skin me twice over.'

'I'm *sorry*. I'd do as much for you, any day. You needn't lie, just say you think I must have met Franz outside.'

'Don't leave your music case here if you want her to believe it.'

I retrieved it hurriedly.

'And what if you run into her going downstairs?'

'I shan't. Not the way I'm going.'

I made my escape via the balcony, making use of the carved wooden beams below. Gina threw my music case down after me and waved goodbye, calling softly, '"A plague on both your houses"!'

I reached the street safely and lurked like a criminal, fearing to face a raging Tommy fresh from her meeting with Ruddigore. I kept my head down and peered into shop windows, watching the reflections of passers-by. Suppose I missed Franz – which way would he come? At last someone loomed up beside me, and his voice greeted me loudly and happily.

I gave a nervous jump. 'Oh, hush.' I grabbed his arm and almost dragged him towards the nearest side street. 'Up here, quick.'

'Some crime you have commit, yes?' Then, more seriously, 'It is not those brutes again, Nell?'

'Oh, no. It's Tommy. I'm not to go out with you today. Oh, do come on, I'll explain later. Have you brought your car?'

'*Natürlich*, it is here by the next corner. I am shopping for food, and – '

'Then I'll linger here while you fetch it, and if you see anyone from my lot drive like stink.'

'Stink?' He wrinkled his brows.

'Fast.' I pushed him. 'Hurry.'

He plunged obediently into the crowd of morning strollers. A few minutes later a horn tooted and his car drew up alongside. It was an open one, old and shabby, but I preferred it instantly to Korbinion's.

'Gina and I are in trouble with Tommy,' I told him as I settled back in my bucket seat and we drove away. 'We went to a restaurant last night with the boys, and – ' I bit my lip. Mustn't make too much of it, not at first; though he would surely hear it all from Peter, later.

'That is all the drama? I am thinking you robbed a bank, at least.'

While he drove, I watched him sideways: was it my imagination, or did he look older and sterner since yesterday? My thoughts flew to that awful demonstration. Instinct told me not to question him; at least, not yet.

'You shiver, Nell? You are cold? In the boot, I have some pully – no, woolovers.'

'I'll have a woolover with pleasure, once we're clear of Innsbruck.' In spite of high summer it was quite chilly in the open car. 'Where are we going, Franz – far?'

'Quite far. A view I would show you. Where you – we – down the Inn look back, and it turns – '

'Winds, you mean?'

'Yes, winds. Mountain, river – *alles so schön ist.*'

'Franz,' I said abruptly, 'that first day, when you wanted to show me round, I never told you – that is, you never asked – '

He frowned. 'Asked? Told me what?'

'That I'd been here before. I have, even to Innsbruck.'

His sigh was like a disappointed child's.

'I – I didn't set out to deceive you.' After last night, it was suddenly very necessary to make this clear. 'I came with my family, never with someone who could show it to me as you do: your own home ground.'

'*So.* Then you even know this road?'

'But only driving towards the town. And then the mountains were hidden in mist, we could just see the river. Anyway, seeing it all with you makes it completely new.'

'Nell,' he said. There was deep satisfaction in his voice. After a moment or so he added happily, 'And the view, today it will be entirely different too. You shall see.'

I've no idea how far we drove. The times we were together always flew, whether we talked or were silent. This drive would have been pure joy if last night's tangle hadn't weighed so on my conscience, the promise that wily Graf Korbinion – impossible to think of him as Korbi – had extracted from me.

At last Franz pulled up by the roadside. 'Do not look back yet, only when I say. *Komm'* – ' We drew the picnic from the boot, with the wine neatly packed in its cooler.

'How very grand,' I exclaimed.

'And it is a grand wine, you will see. Special, for you. It smells of flowers, like your hair.' ('Your hair, Nell, what a pong!' Tim would have said. 'Setting up for Manon Lescaut?')

We walked to the river bank, loaded with woolovers and goodies. Once we had dumped everything on the grass Franz took my arm and turned me to face the other way. 'Now. Is not that special, too?'

The Inn, not the broadest of rivers, took its gently winding course along a green valley sprinkled with flowers and dotted with lazy grazing cattle. Here and there pasture was broken by strung-out villages, marked by bulbous-topped churches and wooden châlets, their balconies heavy with flowers. Distant Innsbruck was hidden now by the lie of the land, but beyond and to either side of the long valley rose mountains, those nearer us more jagged, capped with whiteness even now above the snowline; the farther ones cup-shaped, gently blued by mist in sunlight and shade, all watery like a watercolour. Behind them the giants rose again: the great protecting shield beyond the hidden town.

After a moment Franz jogged my elbow. 'Well?'

'Stupendous; it's – breathtaking. I'm glad it hid last time.'

He seemed satisfied with my response. 'And I, I am glad you feel that, Nell.' Then we were in each other's arms. Franz pulled me roughly down beside him on the ground and kissed me till there were no more thoughts, only longings. I was overwhelmingly happy to think how much he wanted me.

'Franz . . . '

He turned his head aside, murmuring, '*Nicht hier*, Nell. We must not.' I felt only cruel disappointment, and cheated. 'My dearest Franz, why not?'

'We marry, Nell. When it is possible.'

'Yes, ah yes! So why – '

'And there will be many difficulty, obstacles to overcome. We must not hurry, because for you – things could be even harder than for me.'

I didn't want this cautiousness. Only for us to be together, entirely, now. It might be years before we could even dream of marrying. Yet some instinct told me not to urge him then, this moment at least should be his decision. Still, I couldn't resist putting my arms around him, drawing him closer, kissing his neck, his ear, murmuring endearments in English and my highly peculiar German.

'Nell.' He gave a sigh, and sat up suddenly, pulling me with him. He laughed, shakily. 'Behave! Now you have real flowers in your hair – and grass – And look! *Ein Marienkäfer.*' He picked it off. 'See?'

'Ladybird. Isn't she pretty?' I perched the small scarlet and black beetle on my finger, and chanted, '"Ladybird, ladybird, fly away home, your house is on fire and your children are gone."'

Franz said abruptly, 'Nell, did you see the fire last night? *Das Hakenkreuz?* The swastika? You and your friends?'

'Yes, we saw it.' Why have to speak of that vile symbol just now, and last night with all its complications? I put my hand on his arm, drawing him closer again. 'Franz, I didn't enjoy last night – nor did you, I think. Let's not think of ugly things just now. Let's have our unspoilt moment, let's pretend it will last for ever, like this gorgeous place. If things get worse we can gloom at each other, but we'll have had this first, won't we?'

'If it please you, Nell. But I am sorry you were not happy.'

'It was for both of us,' I said truthfully.

He smiled then, as he had smiled at our first meeting.

'Now we will drink to us. *Prost!*'

10

The wine was delicious, flowery. The unpacked hamper revealed succulent chicken in aspic, with truffles; rolls, thickly buttered; and one of those cakes which shape the Teutonic figure, made of sponge and cream and chocolate embedded in more cream.

Emotion didn't spoil our appetites.

'I'm sleepy and happy and fat and happy and sleepy,' I said, after we'd gorged ourselves like puppies. 'All we need now is music.' I leaned back sentimentally against Franz's shoulder, but he pushed me away, rolled over on to his stomach, and reached across to tickle my nose with a grass stem as Tim might have done.

'Fine.' He grinned. 'You sing us something, then.'

'Are you mad? After that meal?' I struck his hand away.

'Now you are cross. You ate too much, perhaps?' He grinned again. 'Come, Nell, do not be cross. Tell me instead what you sing for your third song when you reach semi-finals.'

'Oh . . . "*Heidenröslein*", I suppose. Tommy's favourite. It would be. I hate it, it's so spry and – and yet so bitter. Not what I think of when I remember summer hedges at home full of wild roses.'

'How I would like to see them.'

'You will.'

'Perhaps.'

He plucked another of the flowering grasses and stroked my arm with its trembling tips. '*Liebchen* . . . I have made a –

a translation of your – our Mahler songs. At least, I have finished already *"Liebst du um Schönheit"*. Specially for you. Would you like to hear it?'

'Of course I would, dear egotist.'

He looked crestfallen. I saw it was a mistake to slip into treating him like Tim.

'I was only joking. Honestly. Please tell me.'

He pulled a piece of paper from his pocket, took my hand, and held it while he read:

> Should you love beauty,
> O never love me!
> Love the sun
> He wears fine golden hair!
>
> Should you love youth,
> O never love me!
> Love the springtime
> Returning each year!
>
> Should you love treasure,
> O never love me!
> Love the mermaid
> She has such shining pearls!
>
> Should you love love itself
> Oh yes, then love me!
> Love me for always,
> As I love you always, ever more.

There was silence between us. I had tears in my eyes, for I had walked into a different world; an older, more feeling and mature one than I had known at home. It was impossible to think of Tim or Dan making a translation of that song. Franz's true vein of sentiment must have been developed – like the sterner qualities I sensed in him – by the tough realities of the environment that had brought him early to manhood. What untouched children we must seem to him! What could he see in my untried self? I was afraid that there might be nothing strong enough in me nor generous enough to give him what he needed.

'Nell? You look puzzled. You do not like him – my translation?'

'It's lovely. Simple. I can't judge translations, Franz, but yours is full of the right feeling.'

'Good. Now you owe me something. So sing, yes?'

'I might manage "The Banjo Song". Do you know it? Paul Robeson sings it. That super deep-treacle voice.'

I began to croon:

> I plays the banjo better now
> Than him that taught me to,
> Because he plays for all the world,
> And I jes' plays for you . . .

My voice went too low, I growled. We both collapsed into laughter, 'Pity I haven't Robeson's bass, isn't it? Oh look, Franz – our view, it's misting over.'

The far mountains beyond Innsbruck were lost already. The nearer ones stood out dark against watery whiteness, more like a watercolour than ever.

'Perhaps it rain, soon. Come, Nell, let us pack. Then I take you somewhere to find the little – you know, *Erdbeeren*?'

'Wild strawberries? Heaven.'

A few minutes' drive brought us to the place.

'Come on, greedy Nell.'

'Mmm . . . not sure I could eat anything else just yet. Let's take them back with us instead, souvenir of our perfect day.'

'Perfect for you too?'

'Oh yes. So far.' Some time, I knew, I must make the confession that had been distantly threatening our day like those mountain mists.

Franz's face clouded. 'But you said that as though – '

I put my hand over his mouth. 'Hush, I don't want to talk about it yet.'

We had reached a small clearing beyond a ring of dark fir and mountain ash that hid us from the road. It was very silent here. The trees brooded. I shivered and moved closer to him. Another hour or two of happiness, unspoiled – surely the jealous gods themselves couldn't grudge us that? Then, as Franz turned towards me, I saw for the first time the dark bruise spreading down behind his left ear, the matting of his hair above a graze.

'Where did you get that?' My hand flew out to touch the mark.

'This? Is nothing. Do not look so scared, *Schatz*.'

'The demonstration. That swastika – you were there?'

'Please, it is not serious. But you, Nell, you know it was a demonstration, yes?' He looked at me searchingly.

'Yes, where we were, last night, someone – ' I felt myself redden – 'told me about it, and I was so worried, because of you.'

He didn't speak. Instead, he took me in his arms again. Beneath us the turf was green and inviting. He pulled me down and began kissing me. He was trembling, and I knew his good resolutions were crumbling – while I'd made none, since there was no doubt in me then or any other time that Franz and I belonged together, and if the world were plunging into darkness for the second time we'd every right to snatch whatever happiness we could.

The smell of crushed grass was beneath us, the sun blazed down on us. I lay there utterly content, all senses heightened. Aware of everything, from the minute patterns on the blades of grass to the persistent piping of a hidden bird. For some while we didn't speak, but lay listening to it and the placid flow of a small stream close by.

At last Franz murmured, 'Nell, *du bist so jung, so schön*, I want so much that we marry, but perhaps – '

'Don't, it doesn't matter if we can't marry, nothing does. Only us.'

It was a steep descent from clouds of joy to find real cloud descending in damp streamers of mist, blown by the treacherous mountain winds. I shivered. Arms around each other we returned to the car, and in silence pulled on thicker jerseys. It was only when we were en route that we remembered the wild strawberries.

'No time to pick them now,' said Franz abstractedly.

'No. Your father will be waiting.'

The heavy everyday world was closing in on us, like the mists, dispersing the timelessness we'd just enjoyed. It was my first taste of the cruel jolts that bedevil lovers.

Franz gave me a sideways glance. 'Yes, it is so. And now, the bad news.'

I braced myself. 'Bad . . . for us?'

'My father lose his job.'

'He – but why?' Although I knew.

'All his life he works for one firm, he is a director. Then one day he is sick, he cannot attend – and without him, they vote him from the Board.'

I said clumsily, 'Hasn't he a pension? Nothing at all?'

'But Nell, my father has only fifty years. He does not want to do nothing.'

'I should think not! Is there – can he get something else?'

Franz shook his head. 'You know why. Nell, I have not told him of us. He too upset is, it was not possible. I say only you are a friend from the Contest.'

A few minutes ago our love had seemed unassailable. Somehow the word 'friend' reduced me to insignificance, and I knew the stirrings of fierce resentment against Franz's father, and the damage his despair or plain possessiveness might do. Oh, I must be wise, I thought, holding back angry words, wise for both Franz and myself. He is so young, too. And wished again that I hadn't acted with such lack of wisdom the night before.

'Anyway, your father will leave here now?'

'He says it is our country, they may force him from his job – from the homeland, never.' His foot jabbed at the accelerator.

'Careful! We don't want to end in the river.'

He slowed down, glanced at me again, and said, 'He suggests I leave Austria, Nell.'

My spirits leapt. 'Would you? Would you ever come to us in England?' (I refused to think of what my mother would say.)

Franz's right hand rested on mine a moment, but he didn't answer. 'Shouldn't you both leave, if things are hotting up? I'm sure people who go soon will be the only ones who stand a chance of settling somewhere else – before the rush begins.'

'I told you what my father thinks,' he said, rather haughtily.

And you're too loyal to say you don't agree, I thought with some bitterness. 'You won't desert him then, will you? Whatever he says, because you'll know he doesn't really mean it.'

'Nell, how can I leave him here alone?'

I burst out with, 'But if I can't find a way to stay here – My parents – I'm under age.' And in our path was no ordinary human obstacle but a probable tempest of fire and slaughter. Oh, it was crazy that I was old enough to give myself to Franz, to nurse if war came, but under age to decide my own future.

'We may have to wait. A long, long while, Nell,' said Franz. 'You will wait for me, whatever happen?'

'You know. Always. *"Dich lieb Ich immer, immerdar"*.'

'I too. That is how it is.'

After that, we talked no more. Once I thought, troubled, oh Lord, I never said a word about Korbinion and Bayreuth; too late now. Anyway, a promise extracted like that is no promise. So there's no need to bother Franz with it nor – yet! – with the brewing Tommy row.

His home was on the outskirts of Innsbruck. The car drew up outside a white house with closed windows. Upstairs the blinds were down, as though someone had died. Here, in the ogre's castle, I must try my hardest to charm and I had never felt so charmless. Franz and I walked up the path side by side, we might have been two strangers. It wasn't till we were standing in the porch that he turned to me abruptly, saying once more, 'Nell, *Ich hab' dich gern*.'

I whispered back, 'I love you too,' and followed him into the hall. I felt the house wanted to keep me out, its atmosphere was full of heavy brooding; some old houses at home had that atmosphere, specially Tudor ones, but this house wasn't old.

We walked into the drawing room.

'Wait for me here, Nell? He is perhaps in the garden.'

Franz went away without looking back.

A carved mirror on the wall reflected long green silk curtains, globed lamps, painted furniture, and myself standing in the middle of the room, subdued, alien, English.

Looking at my schoolgirl image I was amazed that such passionate giving had changed me outwardly not at all.

I settled myself on a stiff chair, to wait.

11

'It was a disaster,' I told Gina.

'Oh Nell, you often think people don't like you.'

'You don't understand. I mean, he was too – too upset about things, and monumentally polite like you are to someone you won't see again and don't want to. And he plainly adores Franz. And though he kept talking to him about sending him to America he kept looking at me, and I felt he deliberately didn't say "England"; perhaps he guessed about us. You could tell that he was really latched on to Franz and wanted him to stay – no, *intended* it, underneath.'

'Sure you're not imagining things? Poor man, he must have been feeling pretty awful, anyway. Sad.'

'He was sad, all right – the house vibrated with it. Oh Gina, what am I to do?' I thrust my hands through my hair and looked at her beseechingly.

'After today I should say "best forget Franz altogether".'

'It's just "after today" that I couldn't possibly, ever.'

'Oh, I see. It's been like that, has it?'

'Don't sound so – so condemning.'

'There you go again. I'm just madly jealous. One huge great female jealousy. It must really change things.'

'It could certainly change *me*.' I began to cry, and she put her arms round me consolingly.

'Darling, don't.'

I wiped my eyes drearily, and tried to smile.

'And now Tommy. Was she simply terrible?'

'Wow! Rampaging all over the place about Disgraceful

Pupils – as if anyone would bother, except her. In fact, love, we'd be on the night train home if it weren't for Prince Charming.'

'Who?'

'You can't have forgotten Herr Mejor Graf Korbinion and his glass-slipper complex? He actually turned up here in the middle of the row and asked to see her, oozing charm. Probably guessed we wouldn't get away with it. Even Tommy calmed down and began purring when she learned that the Princess is his aunt. Well, you know our Tommy, howling snob, and Music has no Frontiers. Anyway, the precious Princess has been prevailed on by said Graf to ask you to Bayreuth so he can lead you by the hand up the famous Green Hill, with a hey-nonny-nonny and a hotcha-cha.'

I gaped at her in consternation. Korbinion must also have guessed I'd back out, and had smoothly gone to work. Opposition would egg him on, he was the type.

'I *can't*, Gina. That promise was dragged out of me. I haven't told Franz; I was just determined not to go.'

'If you'd won seats you'd have gone like a rocket.'

'With Franz.'

'Could he – without trouble?'

'I don't know,' I said, more wretchedly. 'Anyway, G., my father wouldn't like me to go to Germany.'

'Didn't seem to worry you about Bayreuth before.'

I collapsed on to a bed as though my legs had given way. Gina put an arm around my shoulders again. 'Buck up, do. What's so bad about it, after all? I'd give my eyes to see part of the "Ring" there, or *Parsifal.*' As I just sat with my head in my hands, she added, 'If you think Franz would be upset, tell him the Princess has taken a fancy to you. Don't mention the fascinating Korbi.'

'Fascinating! Do you suppose he's the type to hide his light under a bushel?' I said bitterly. 'Don't you realize he was probably controlling that whole swastika affair the other night, where Franz got hurt? It would all get round to Franz somehow. I won't go on deceiving him, it would be fatal.'

But Gina was relentless. 'It's Bayreuth for you, or straight home for the four of us. That won't help you either, will it? And you can jolly well think of Tim and Dan and me too, and be reasonable about dear Korbi – he can't eat you.'

I groaned. '*Et tu, Brute*! Maybe I can escape it somehow, later.'

'Don't be a goose, you'll enjoy it. He's very attractive. I think you've got in too fast with Franz altogether, if you don't mind my saying so. There seems no future in it. By the way, you're having coffee with Tommy and the Princess this evening.'

I gave a second and louder groan.

'So. The young girl my nephew wish I shall invite.' The Princess's shrewd grey eyes pierced like needlepoints.

With Tommy watching me and the Princess examining me through her lorgnette I felt six years old. To my annoyance I was blushing.

'Charming. A little gauche, perhaps. The dress is impossible. You sing tomorrow, child?'

'My solos in the afternoon. Choir in the evening,' I muttered.

'So? Then in the morning I shall have you fitted for something more suitable. Bayreuth is an occasion, the first "Ring" cycle is honoured by the Führer.'

She waited for my response. I made none.

'Eleanor is quite overcome by the honour your Highness does her. Thank the *Fürstin*, Eleanor. It will be an occasion to remember always.'

I forced out something inadequate, and mumbled that my father would expect to pay for any new clothes.

'Your father would like you to accept gifts graciously, Eleanor,' said Tommy.

I meant to add that he wouldn't want me to go to Germany; but in the face of the Princess's overpowering presence, with Tommy at her side, I was struck dumb.

'*Ausgezeichnet!* Is settled. Now, what do you sing?'

I told her. 'And "*Heidenröslein*", if I reach the next round.'

'Well, Fräulein Armstrong, I must wish you both luck.' The Princess rose, monumental in grey silk. Her white hair in heavy bands framed a weatherbeaten face innocent of the make-up that Hitler was said to disapprove. 'You will see me at the Hall. No, do not rise – ' (but Tommy did, with a curious bowing movement of her neck) – 'and, child, we shall be meeting in the dress shop tomorrow. At eleven. Frau Monika's – Madame Monique, she calls herself, what nonsense. Your teacher will doubtless be occupied elsewhere. Do not be late.'

Much against my will I found myself mesmerized into curtseying. Her hand seized my chin and jerked it up.

'Straighten, straighten – is better so. You English should pay attention to detail, as we do in Germany.' She patted my head, the final humiliation. 'So, little one. You will enjoy the glories of our great Master, who so amply express our national spirit.' She left us abruptly, without Heil Hitling. Perhaps she kept it for her own land. Or perhaps, with luck, she was so grand and important that she didn't have to do it. Tommy was beaming as if she'd seen the Beatific Vision. Grandeur and Wagner together had ousted all thoughts of the Nazi régime.

'Like stags it will be,' said Tim with relish. 'Shall I take on the winner? Bet it's the amorous and powerful Graf. Think, our divine Lorelei carried off to one of those twisted castles, all pepperpots and oubliettes, and wild boar for breakfast. Or it's Count Drac's toothmarks. Let's have a bob on the result.'

'Don't tease her, Tim,' said Gina. 'Poor Nell's been cornered.'

We had retreated to our room and the boys had slipped up the back stairs to join us, in spite of my attempt to shut the door on them.

'Tommy can't send us home for this, wouldn't want the Princess to know, would she?' argued Dan.

'Now you're here, can't you help me? *Think* of something.'

Gina shook her head. 'You're stuck with it, Nell. Better make a clean breast to Franz as soon as possible.'

'He'll think I'm a mass of deceit,' I said miserably. 'I only told him today that I'd been here before.'

'Must learn about women some time, poor old lad,' said Tim. 'But, Nell, I've thought of something: introduce me to the old trout, and I'll *küss die Hand* and make up to her till she invites me too.'

'That wouldn't look so bad to Franz, would it?' approved Gina.

I thought it over. Certainly it would look better if I weren't just one of a trio with the Princess and her forthcoming nephew. 'Don't see how you'll manage it, though.'

'Old family friend, much like brother,' suggested Tim. 'Better still, first cousin. Is Tommy going to this dress shop too?'

'Oh no, the Princess threw out strong hints against it.'

'Fine. Then it's just right for you to be escorted by your courteous coz, and ta-ra-ra! Watch me do my stuff. Cross your fingers and put your faith in Uncle.'

'Attaboy,' said Dan.

An enormous Mercedes with a uniformed chauffeur stood outside the shop. A nearby clock chimed the hour as we approached.

'On your marks, Nell. Ready for the land of vulgar riches?'

Inside the shop the Princess spread like a blancmange on the only comfortable chair, with Frau Monika, dressed in elegant black, fussing round her. My feet sank into deep pile, my nose took in a delicate flowerscented atmosphere. Tim bowed, and I bent my knees as though hypnotized. The Princess raised her lorgnette to favour him with a pale blue aristocratic stare.

In my best German I introduced Tim as my cousin.

The harsh features softened. 'Good, you attempt German, child; but we will speak English, mine is excellent, we have a talent for other tongues not possessed by our Anglo-Saxon cousins. So this young man is your cousin? I did not know families accompany the singers? Wait! I have seen him in the choir.' She held out a large mottled hand which Tim reverently kissed.

'*Fürstin*,' he murmured, sounding so awestruck that I had to repress my giggles.

'Nell and I are like brother and sister,' volunteered Tim. 'My uncle wouldn't let her come abroad without me.'

Don't overdo it, I begged him inwardly.

'You have pretty manners, young man. Unlike some youth today.'

Tim looked gratified. 'When shall I return for Nell?'

'Return? My dear boy, it is only a step to her *Gasthof*.'

'But Miss Armstrong was cross when I took her out without permission the other night. So I ought to see her home.' He looked earnest and appealing.

The Princess gave a surprisingly jolly laugh. 'In that case I shall – how is it in English? Drop her out. You too. Wait, then, and see your cousin's choice, Timothy.' She heaved herself out of her chair. 'Frau Monika will show us what is suitable.' She preceded us up some shallow steps. Although it was so hot she was swathed in sables, clasped above her shoulder by a pair of anguished animal masks. Half-way up she turned to press a vast leather bag into Tim's arms. 'So. My new gentleman-in-waiting.' He received it as though it held manna from heaven.

In the salon we sat ourselves down on three spindle-legged chairs. A magnificent Venetian chandelier hung from the ceiling, and the carpet pile was even deeper here. It must be a very expensive place indeed.

'Now, Frau Monika! The Fräulein accompanies me to Bayreuth. An occasion for her, you understand. Show us what you have for the daytime, the reception, the Opera.'

I spluttered, 'But it – it was evening dress only, I thought.'

I might not have spoken.

'The *Fürstin* favours a special colour?'

'What colour, Eleanor? . . . No, not green. Blue is for young girls, also pink. And for the evening, white: you may look well in white. A pity that you have short hair. Frau Monika, I am waiting.' The Princess dragged off her sables and piled them on top of the bag already crowning Tim's knees.

Madame flew to obey. Model after model began twirling before us, then reappeared in other garments. I soon stopped offering my opinion, since the Princess knew hers. She sat with sturdy legs apart, mottled hands on knees, pince-nez replacing the lorgnette. Sometimes she snapped out an order. I glanced at Tim for support but he was staring soulfully ahead.

The last dress was modelled for us.

'Now go with Frau Monika and try on the ones we picked together, child. Then come back here to show us the result.'

At last: 'Make a note of that blue silk coat and skirt for daytime, Frau Monika. Lengthened. Her knees are so – what is it, Eleanor?'

'Isn't it a bit young?' I said helplessly. It was tremendously ship ahoy. Tim was choking into the sables. I couldn't blame him, since I felt irresistibly like a sea cadet, adorned with brass buttons and a sailor collar.

'Nonsense, you are young. It is very well made.'

'It's – rather naval.'

'You, an Englishwoman, would complain of that? You will wear your boater with it. Is there not a Royal Yacht, Timothy?'

'Yes, "Britannia". Nell looks just like Young Britannia now. I love it.'

'This young man is a patriot.' She beamed on him. 'Take her away, Frau Monika, let us see something girlish for the Reception. That pretty pink one.'

Two assistants attired me in it before I was paraded again, cocooned like a simpering birthday doll in layers of crêpe de chine, flounced and ruffled and bowed and embroidered in all shades of pink from neck to hem.

'Extremely suitable, we will take it.' I began to wonder if she was hoping to put her nephew off me.

'Not *Heidenröslein* exactly,' said Tim. 'Perhaps the last rose of summer.'

'Make a note, Frau Monika: elbow-length pink gloves.' Tim choked again. I glared at him. 'Bronze dancing pumps, which never date. They will be useful for her later.'

'When she's twenty-one.' Tim leered at me sideways.

'We keep no shoes here,' Madame was saying.

'You will certainly send out for them. Do not forget to take the size of Fräulein Dobell's hands and feet, they are not small.'

From Madame, meekly, 'It is understood, *Ihr Hochheit*.'

Seething, I paid small attention to the evening dress that an assistant flung over my head, although it was an agreeable surprise: white silk chiffon, scattered with pearl and crystal towards the hem. At least it might make up for the humiliation of Last Rose and Ship Ahoy.

'Charming,' said the Princess. 'My full approval. We need see no more, eh, Timothy? What do you think, young man?'

'You're absolutely right, Princess. From cabbage rose to cabbage butterfly.'

'Again, long gloves. White. And white court shoes, Frau Monika. The account to me, the clothes to Fräulein Dobell at her *Gasthof*.'

When I re-emerged from the dressing room Frau Monika had disappeared, and the Princess and Tim were too absorbed in conversation to notice my return. I stretched disbelieving ears.

' – I always understood the sons of English lords were sent to Eton or to – *ach* – Arrow, not so?'

'But my father was a younger son, like Nell's. So, not much of the ready, er – cash. Anyway, Eton was out of the question for me: weak chest. College by the river, and all that.'

'My dear boy, how unfortunate! Tradition is so important.'

'My parents felt it,' said Tim solemnly. 'Still, I'm lucky to have gone to school where I can sing in the same choir as Nell, aren't I?'

'And does Eleanor suffer from this – weakness too?' An appraising glance at me.

'Not Nell! She's strong as an ox. And singing's done me a lot of good. Expands the chest. Queen Mary said so to my grandfather only the other day.'

'The dear Queen! Infinitely gracious. She came with his late Majesty to try the waters at Bad Kissingen.' The Princess turned to me and patted my hand. 'Eleanor told me nothing of all this. With us, it is appreciated, that a young woman should be so modest. And docile. Now, Eleanor, my dear, you and this young man shall lunch with me and tell me more about yourselves.'

'But it's my quarter-final this afternoon,' I said faintly. 'And I must practice first, and Miss Armstrong has arranged a light lunch for me.'

'*Schade*, but you will see my nephew later, he takes special leave. Timothy will certainly lunch with me. I need my new gentleman-in-waiting, you see. And we will talk of Wagner.'

'Great,' said Tim. 'If Nell wins tickets I'm coming to Bayreuth with them.'

The Princess snorted, a full definite snort, such as Brünhilde's horse might have given. 'Tickets! Such nonsense. We shall talk of that too. But first to drop out Miss Eleanor at her *Gasthof*.'

Half-way downstairs Tim turned and gave me an enormous wink.

'Maniac!' I whispered. 'Bet she keeps a row of – of Debrett and all that sort of thing by her bed.'

'Not here, surely? I beg your pardon, *Fürstin*? Yes, we do look forward to seeing Graf Korbinion, don't we, Nell, it will make our day. Absolutely.'

'Do you realize you've turned me into a suitable bride?' I hissed.

'Specially in that stunning pink. Not to worry, it won't last, and I'm already half-way to Bayreuth.'

No use speaking to Tim when he was in full complacent fantasy. Glowering, I joined the Princess in her car.

'Thank you for that lovely evening dress,' I forced myself to say.

She inclined her head. 'I am fond of Korbinion. Winifred Wagner was lately telling me the Führer himself has great feeling for the English.'

I was speechless.

'Then he'll certainly appreciate our healthy docile English rose,' said Tim, handing her into her sables.

'Damn Tim! Damn him, damn him, damn him,' I exploded.

'You'll bring up that light lunch, if you're not careful,' said Gina. 'What happened – didn't he succeed?'

'Succeed? He got off with her, that's all. Rushed off to lunch with her to have a jolly chat about Wagner.'

'That's what you wanted, isn't it? Clever old Tim.'

'Gina, he's told her packs of lies about our royal-blue blood, and she's come over all graciously matrimonial. Don't just sit there laughing, I could murder you too. Listen: Tommy told me to wait for her, but I'm dashing down to the Hall early, I simply must see Franz before the *Hochgeboren* close in on me again.'

12

'Oh Franz, I must speak to you!'

The quick glance he gave over his shoulder reminded me of the threatening shadows. 'No one tries to harm you, Nell?'

I shook my head. 'Over by the window, quick – before Tommy gets here. Listen – '

To my own ears my stumbling confession of Korbinion's interest sounded sly and trivial. 'It all began that awful swastika night,' I wound up. 'The next evening was terrible, because only that wretched man's wretched aunt saved Gina and me from being sent home to England. And, Franz, I was going to tell you about him yesterday, only I didn't want to spoil things . . . we were so terribly happy. And then you were so worried about what happened to your father. But once I got myself involved with that silly party of Gina's the whole Bayreuth thing simply snowballed.'

Franz put his hand on my arm. 'Nell, you do not trust me?'

'But of course I do.'

'Then why so much fear?'

My relief was huge. 'You don't mind, then?'

'Yes, I mind. I mind you are unhappy – that you involve yourself with this man. There are so many like him, too proud to be Party members and so useful to the Nazis as they are. That sort, for a thousand year they survive, believe me they know how.' His voice had hardened. 'Nell, best you refuse to go, whatever happen.'

I was aghast. 'That could mean not seeing you again.'

'You must risk it.'

'Never! Now you understand, I can stick it out. Anyway, Tommy's making me go, to please the *Fürstin*.'

'She would please a Nazi?' He sounded incredulous.

'She's pleased a princess. *And* she believes music is a force for good.'

'Not always Wagner. And her nephew was at the – the demonstration.' His voice was sombre. 'He told you this?'

'He only said he was sent to see it was controlled,' I said hastily.

'He arrives not too early, not too late. He is clever. So, he keeps Nazi trust and Austrian trust.' Franz's hand strayed unconsciously to the ugly marks on his neck.

I touched them gently.

'Oh, my darling, I wouldn't go to Bayreuth with him for any gold, if I could stay here otherwise.'

'Could you not be ill, perhaps?'

'Deceive Tommy in that way? Even Gina doesn't manage it.'

'Then I shall come too. Somehow, Nell, I get tickets. Or if you win, I take yours, *ja*?'

'Franz, it would be dangerous for you.'

'Yet it is a promise?'

I was saved from answering by Tommy. 'Eleanor! So here you are. You were to wait for me and Dan at the *Gasthof*.' Her expression was glacial. She ignored Franz's presence.

He murmured in my ear, 'I am singing last. When do you?'

'Second. I'll wait for you.'

Nothing escaped Tommy. She sniffed. 'Graf Korbinion is here with his aunt. Naturally they expect you to sit with them.'

'But surely the Adjudicators wouldn't like that?' And I made one last plea: 'Miss Armstrong, my father didn't expect me to go to Germany, couldn't you explain that?'

'Nonsense, child. You were anxious to go if you won tickets, I remember that clearly. Your father would understand my not wishing to offend the Princess for the choir's sake. Besides, she's Bavarian, the highly respected patron of this Contest, no possible harm can come to you with her. The experience will be good for you, away from – ' a glance at Franz – 'other students.'

The first contestant had sung unnoticed by us; somebody was shouting my name.

'Viel Glück, Nell, mein Herz.'

As I preceded Dan on to the dais I made the mistake of looking at the audience, where a bulky figure sat by a spare and elegant one. Before my eyes swam a monstrous vision of the pink rose dress. I halted.

'Nell,' hissed Dan, giving me a push.

'Liebst du um Schönheit' was my first song, as it had been before. I was aware of singing it with some lack of assurance, because Franz's English words kept intruding on my memory. But when it came to 'Where Corals Lie' I wallowed in Elgar's lush sentimentality, and Dan backed me nobly as I left the purple passage of 'sunset-glowing lips' behind, and reached the last repeated ' – where corals lie'.

There was a storm of genuine applause. I knew that I would never have sung so well if worrying about Franz and Korbinion hadn't swamped all fear of failure.

Back in the artists' room fat little Irma came up to me effusively, but I soon grew aware of someone else hovering in the doorway, and her flow was interrupted.

'Nell, it is possible to speak with you? I bring a message from my aunt.'

I avoided Franz's eyes, and walked out reluctantly into the passage. Korbinion put his hand on my arm to draw me further off, but I resisted, determined to stay where we could be seen.

'We were impressed. You truly have a voice. Aunt Greta sends me to fetch you now.'

'Please thank the Princess, but I can't come.'

Korbinion looked nonplussed. 'Can't? Why is that?'

'I'm a competitor, and your aunt's a patron.'

'Ah, so this is just an English sense of fair play?'

'Don't you still have one in Germany?'

He looked amused, which was somehow disquieting. 'A sharp-tongued *Mädchen*! May I say that Miss Armstrong saw no harm in the suggestion?'

'She's rather silly, sometimes. Is Tim – my cousin – with the Princess still?'

'Your cousin. Is he, indeed? How interesting.' He seemed more amused. I was very conscious of Franz watching us. 'Yes, she finds Timothy quite charming, he comes with us to Bayreuth too. Now, Nell, I will tell Aunt Greta that you'll drink tea with us, later. I come myself to collect you, do not run away.' His smile was over-sweet.

I returned to Franz, who was scowling.

Irma said: 'That was *der Herr Graf*. The – the nephew of – *die Fürstin*.' Her little eyes were sharp as a challenge.

'Franz?' I whispered. 'It's not my fault.' He managed a reassuring smile.

Like a child, I promised myself that if he sang his Mahler song really well today it would be a good omen, things would work out for us. It seemed a long while to wait before he and Peter walked on to the dais. I clenched my fists, till I heard his voice ring out and was spellbound by its rich deep tone:

Ich bin der Welt abhanden gekommen –

'Der Mahler, er war auch Jude,' said Irma.

Mahler was also a Jew. I hadn't thought of that, and didn't know whether to applaud Franz for his audacity or shudder at the strength which sooner or later was bound to make him tangle with the authorities . If only I could spirit him away to England, keep him safe there, keep us both safe. Tears filled my eyes.

Now Franz was beginning *'Abschied'*. He performed it brilliantly, while Peter's fingers struck out the hurried trotting rhythm with a speed and accuracy that drew frenzied applause for them both. I jumped to my feet and went to meet them in the archway. They were thumping each other on the back and looked flushed and happy. I hated to break the spell.

'Oh, Franz, the Mahler . . . perfect! Listen, though,' I added nervously, 'the Princess has asked me to tea, Tommy too, with the nephew.' The thunderclouds returned; I saw elation change to bleakness. 'Rescue me! The second the judging's over we must slip out, although Tommy will be livid.'

Franz nodded. He drew out his car keys and pressed them into my hand. 'It is round at the back. Your name comes before mine; go the moment you can, yes?'

I agreed, casting all thoughts of *Fürstin*-reactions to the winds, and returned to my seat, aware of Irma's scrutiny. Once Franz leaned across to ask me, 'The Mahler – you truly liked?' And I answered, 'Beautiful, just right,' thrusting Irma's spiteful comment from my mind.

We hadn't long to wait for the results. The moment my name had been called, I hurried outside to Franz's car. Soon he rejoined me.

'Nell, I am glad for you. But me – I am out.'

'You sang superbly, better than anyone,' I said hotly.

'I know.' He gave a bitter laugh, and started the car, crashing the gears. I saw how much he minded; at least he didn't mind my seeing it. 'I told you how it would be, Nell: so far, and then – out.' He forced a smile. 'Now, we try to forget all this. I take you to a café where the elegant von und zu will not go.'

It was on the river bank, quiet and almost empty, except for two or three workmen with their girls.

We sat together on a bench, eating slices of cake and drinking tall tumblers of coffee, rich with cream.

'Why is food such a comfort when one's sad?'

'Return to the mother, says Freud.' His smile was sweet.

I laughed. 'Not my mother, I assure you.'

'Do not be sad, Nell. Not for me.'

'You are me, don't you understand that yet?'

'Nell, *Ich hab' dich gern.*'

Tears pricked behind my eyes. I put my hand over his on the table. 'Look, let's make a plan: a plan of escape for you. Have you a pen here? Write my address down now, before you forget.'

'I would never forget.' But he obeyed, while adding, 'But we have just this moment, Nell. The present. And, if we are lucky, a very far-off future.'

The certainty in his voice appalled me.

'Not far-off. Soon,' I insisted.

'If Hitler permit.'

'If there's a miracle, then. Why doesn't your father force you to leave? He could.' (Selfish old man, I almost added.) And I pleaded once again, 'Now's the time for you *and* him, before Hitler marches and frontiers are closed – isn't that what happens?'

'Probably, though not just yet. Nell, what could he do in England?'

'What can he do here? And how long will Jews get pensions if – ?'

Franz pressed my hand fiercely. 'Please not, Nell. And what would I do in England or America?'

'Sing. You've an amazing voice.'

'I need years of training.'

'In England you could train and earn at the same time, you could – translate! You're almost bi-lingual.'

'That would not keep two of us, or – Finish the cake, Nell. I am not hungry now. And – ' he smiled wrily – 'win Bayreuth tickets for me, yes?'

'You'd be in danger there,' I said reluctantly. 'Anyway, Tim's coming too, he'll ride off the Graf.'

'I am already in danger, you know that. Now perhaps in worse – of losing you too, Nell.'

'To *Korbinion*? What rot.'

'That, I could not bear,' he said. 'Tell me, what are the

plans for tomorrow, Sunday?'

I grimaced. 'Tommy – damn her! – has arranged church and then an all-day coach outing. No exceptions whatever allowed. I tried.'

'What a waste for us, Nell. Yet I should stay home, to cheer my father. It is not easy.'

'Monday morning we're singing again. I am, anyway. Then I'm free.'

'Shall we go to the mountains, then? With Peter and Gina?'

'Must we take them?'

'It is better so. Towards Germany there are thugs and – and bears in the mountains, have you not heard?' He smiled, but his tone was serious.

'I'll do anything you say, because we must have Monday, Franz. Oh Lord, we'd better go back, I suppose. Whatever excuse can I give the Princess? Sick from nerves?'

'I corrupt you, I think.' He looked at me sombrely. 'Did you lie so before, *mein Herz?*'

'Dearest Franz, the choice is between pleasing her and being sent home. And no, but there was nothing worth lying for.'

Korbinion's charm barely concealed underlying sulks. The Princess was frosty, though soon thawed by Tim's 'Poor Nell, public solos always make her sick', or by our mythical connection with the peerage. Tommy had already left to supervise the juniors. Tim walked me home, describing the way in which he had adroitly steered the Princess off our lofty lineage over tea. 'Although Tommy must know all England's descended from Edward the Third. Anyway, though she may find out what I said, and scalp us, she'd never dare tell the Princess that it wasn't true, would she?'

I made some noncommittal reply; I was thankful that Franz had not been there, to see the ease with which Tim was lying too.

13

We sang well that evening. With Franz still singing in his choir, and Korbinion recalled to duty, I gave myself up to the pleasures of music. There was tough competition, especially from a small French choir which charmed everyone with Mendelssohn – 'Lift thine eyes to the mountains' – and '*Bonjour, mon coeur*' by Orlando di Lassus. But it was the home team who had the edge on us all; they sang Bach, followed by a brilliant performance of Pergolesi's *Stabat Mater*.

When the results were announced I wasn't surprised to hear Franz's choir placed first for their 'very persuasive renderings' and 'lovely texture and blend of tone.' A few minutes later Tommy was beaming to hear our own singing described as 'rhythmically vital' with a 'subtle variety of tone shading.'

So, from those of us who sang that night, we and the Austrians were chosen for the semi-finals.

'Thank God that's over,' said Gina, and added almost pityingly, 'Perfect love casteth out fear! You don't worry about anything at all these days except Franz, do you, love?'

'And Korbinion and his aunt.'

'Oh, come on! You're okay now for Bayreuth, with Tim.'

'Mmm. But Franz swears he's coming to Bayreuth too.'

'You don't *want* him to?'

'Oh, for pity's sake, G.! To the heart of Nazi Germany?'

'He's Austrian, they can't touch him.'

I just looked at her. I could see she didn't understand. In

these last days a world of experience divided us.

Together we went through to the foyer. Franz was in a far corner, buttonholed by his choirmaster. Herr Schmidt was in full flow. Someone came up behind us and took my arm.

'Ah, Nell, what pleasure. My congratulations, again.' Korbinion raised my hand and kissed it in a proprietary way.

'Oh. I thought you'd gone back to Germany.'

'Did I not say I took leave?'

Just then Irma popped up beside us. 'El-ean-or! *Heinrich und Ich*, we have ticket won for *Siegfried*.' She was staring pointedly at Korbinion, so I introduced them and gladly escaped with Gina to see the results of the draw. My name was there. An envelope pinned beside it contained tickets for *Siegfried* and *Götterdämmerung*. I stuffed them hurriedly into my pocket, hoping Franz hadn't seen. Unfortunately, Korbinion had. He was hovering at my elbow, having ruthlessly rid himself of Irma.

He said loudly, 'So, you are successful, Nell? Well, you do not need tickets now. Doubtless one of your friends will benefit. Fräulein Gina, perhaps?'

Gina looked embarrassed, gazing over my shoulder.

'Nell,' said Franz's voice.

I turned, feeling furious with Korbinion, and with myself for not finding some way of snubbing him.

'Hello, Franz. I was coming to find you, but Herr Schmidt got there first.' He was staring, as Irma had, at Korbinion. This time I was reluctant to make the introduction. I was so confused I hardly knew what I was saying. 'You haven't met – Graf Korbinion – '

'But the Herr Mejor and I *have* met.'

'I'm afraid I have no recollection of it.' Korbinion said it pleasantly enough, but there was something false about his tone.

'No, Herr Mejor? The night of the swastika – when one of your friends hit me with his club?' Franz had dropped into German, and Korbinion answered in the same way, 'You mistake. Those young toughs are not my friends.'

'I'm sorry if I got the wrong impression. They're not of the right class?'

Oh, Franz, I prayed silently, *don't* –

'Class?' Korbinion raised his eyebrows. 'We are of different rank – and views.'

'You just give the orders, then – and stay out of range?'

For a moment I feared Korbinion was going to hit him. He smiled unpleasantly. 'Believe me, I'm sorry if you were hurt, but emotional students should learn to keep out of trouble and mind their books. We have young fire-eaters too, at Heidelberg.'

'Fireraisers, too, perhaps? It's not so easy to stay out of trouble, Herr Mejor, when it invades one's country.'

'Forgive me, I do not think all Austrians share your opinion that it comes from outside.'

'Could you both stop behaving as if Gina and I weren't here?' I said desperately. 'Tommy's waiting for us, Franz.'

'Be quiet, Nell, this is serious, and – '

'Being rude to Fräulein Nell is really serious,' said Korbinion in mockery. 'The good Herr Schmidt will also be waiting for his erring pupil.' His tone relegated Franz to the status of a silly five-year-old. 'Nell, I must go too: I have not escaped all duties this week-end. Will you come out with me on Monday? I can drive over again. We must some little plans for Bayreuth make, you know.'

'Monday, she sings – and then *we* are going out together. Nell, you won those tickets?'

I gave Franz a warning look, while Korbinion turned to Gina. 'Fräulein, we may have the great pleasure of seeing *you* at Bayreuth?' He kissed our hands ceremoniously, held mine longer than was necessary, then kissed its palm. I snatched it away. He smiled. '*Auf wiedersehen*, then, till you have your little holiday between semi-final and finals day. Then my aunt will whisk you away like a fairy godmother to our wicked land of Wagner's myths – '

'And H-Hitler's atrocities,' stammered Franz in cold fury.

Korbinion easily ignored him. 'Perhaps we shall never let you go,' he said teasingly, 'unless some young Siegfried or Walther comes to rescue you from dragonland.'

'But Siegfried got the wicked Hagen's spear in the back, didn't he?' put in Gina.

'Nell has saucer-eyes, I do believe she thinks my second name is Hagen!' Korbinion sketched a salute which managed to exclude Franz, and was gone, running down the steps to an official car. Franz watched his histrionic departure, fuming.

'Uniforms! How they love them.'

Gina tactfully moved away, leaving us together.

'How dare he drool over you, Nell? And you would not give me the tickets.' He looked hurt. 'Westerhausern is an arrogant bastard. Do not go, *mein Herz*, please.'

'I *have* to,' I said miserably. 'I could call my father and ask him to forbid it – but then Tommy would send me home. If only the gap between the last singers' heats didn't fit so well with the two last operas in the "Ring".' My hand closed on the tickets in my pocket. 'Please, Franz, keep away from Bayreuth! I'm afraid. You've got across him already, and now he'll guess there's something between us.'

Franz's eyes darkened. 'And how he "got across" me too. If you think fear of any Herr Mejor Graf von und zu will keep me away, you mistake. The tickets, Nell.' Weakly, I obeyed. 'Don't look so unhappy. Everyone should know there is something between us – I want to shout it.'

'You almost did.'

'And that annoyed *you*? Perhaps you want to please the charming Graf?'

'Of course I don't. But it's so dangerous for you to make open enemies.'

'Sometimes one must make open choice,' said Franz stiffly. 'And you should put finish to that man's pursuit.'

'Trust me, Franz – can't you see I'm trying to? Only

opposition excites him, it's his beastly boar-hunting ancestors.'

'Walter,' said Herr Schmidt beside us.

'I come. *Zum Montag*, Nell.'

Before I could say another word we were swept apart by our respective choirs. I was close to tears.

'Oh, that was terrible, G.'

'Cheer up, duckie.'

'How can I, when Franz won't see that Tommy pulls the strings? No, that's unfair, he just says I should risk being sent home rather than stay with the Princess. Perhaps he thinks Tommy would relent, but he doesn't know her. Anyway, I'm not going to be anyone's pretty pink *Püppchen*. I'll give that awful rose dress to Anna, she could use the silk. My best school dress is good enough for any silly reception.'

Gina opened her mouth to speak, then shut it again. I was too worried to ask her what she'd meant to say.

Sunday was a grey day, filled for me with gloom, church, and our boring coach outing. Semi-finals day dawned gloriously: the skies were summer blue, the mountains basked in splendour.

Barred from competing himself, Franz came down to the Hall to hear me sing. I had wanted to withdraw after the Adjudicators' decision, but Tommy wouldn't hear of it.

'Don't be silly, Eleanor. Just because you have a crush on this boy you're imagining all sorts of things that may be far from the truth. There could be many reasons why they failed him, which you do not understand. You are musically immature, as well as in other ways.'

I longed to say that I was no longer so immature as she thought me, but managed to restrain myself. However, though Tommy failed me, I could still publicly show my solidarity with Franz, and I bullied Dan till he agreed to help.

'Okay, you lunatic, but it will probably ditch us both. I'll have to sightread, and I think they've got a list of what you'll sing.'

We began with the Elgar, and my second song was *'Liebst du um Schönheit'*. It was quite the wrong order, and I was careful not to catch Tommy's eye. When we had finished I took a deep breath to steady myself, stepped forward on the dais, and said as clearly as possible, 'I was going to sing Schubert's *"Heidenröslein"*, but I am changing to the final song in the Mahler cycle, *"Ich bin der Welt abhanden gekommen"*. It was sung in the earlier heats by an Austrian student who failed the quarter-final, and I should like to sing it for you now instead.'

I stepped back, gave Franz a tremulous smile – he was sitting in the front row – and looked at Dan to show that I was ready. Goodness, I thought, as he began to play, this must be exactly how they felt before the tumbrils came for them . . .

Afterwards, waiting for the results, Tommy was so angry that it would have been straight to the station with me if it hadn't been for the Princess and Bayreuth. 'That was provocative and stupid, Eleanor. I would never have let you make that change, and well you know it! We're not here to play at politics, and even if it's not looked on in that light your action has probably failed you – which you amply deserve. You hardly know that song, and Dan played it atrociously. Where did he get the music?'

I said as meekly as possible, 'I have sung it quite often at home, Miss Armstrong. And I had the whole song cycle with me, in my case.' But I could barely repress my pleasure, for Franz was plainly delighted, and any constraint between us since that scene with Korbinion had vanished.

In the event, I hadn't failed. Perhaps the Adjudicators, unaware of my involvement with Franz, had seen my gesture merely as one of pleasure in the song. But I knew Tommy was right about my singing of it, and I was lucky to scrape through. My success softened her anger, and after lunch, while Gina and I were waiting for Franz and Peter to collect us, she drew me aside to ask if I had written to my family. I shook my head.

'Then I will send a note to your father today, telling him of your success. I shall tell him too that I'm releasing you from the choir till you return from your little holiday with the Princess – it will be a good opportunity for him to learn of her kind invitation. I'm sure he likes to hear everything about his daughter's progress.'

I almost asked her if my 'progress' included Korbinion; but it was never wise to twist Tommy's tail too far, and there was always the chance that she might retaliate at once by forbidding me after all to go with Franz to the mountains, even though Gina and Peter were coming too.

14

'Is that your only luggage, Eleanor?' asked the Princess. 'There should be a third box from Frau Monika, surely? She cannot have packed two dresses together.' She raised her voice. 'Timothy! Go and find this stupid porter. No, no, Eleanor, sit still. All is soon clear.'

Tim leaped from the car with maddening speed, and soon returned carrying the abominable pink dress. He gave me his sweetest smile. 'Poor crazy Nell hung it in her wardrobe. I couldn't find the box.'

'Tell my chauffeur to put it in the boot, and over it a rug. That is right. Get in, Timothy, we are already late.'

The Mercedes glided forward. I sat crushed between my two companions, and managed to mutter in Tim's ear, 'Beast. I promised it to Anna.'

'The Princess would have sent back for it,' he whispered. 'Anyway, it's bound to put old Korbi off you.'

'What's that? Without a pretty dress Eleanor could not come to Wahnfried, it would not be possible,' said the Princess.

'Wahnfried?'

'Wahnfried is the Wagner family home. Winifred Wagner, the widow of the Master's son, arranges everything – she *is* the Festival. In her grounds, the Führer Reception will be held – naturally, since the Führer himself is her intimate friend, and stays at the Wahnfried annexe during the first "Ring" cycle. Of course we already miss *Rheingold* – and *Walküre* today – because of our own *Musikfest, nicht wahr,* little one?' She patted my hand jovially. 'A pity, but I am, after all, a Patron. Still, tomorrow we have the pause in the cycle, and a Reception.'

'You mean we, Tim and I, are invited – '

'*Aber natürlich*, you are my guests. Winifred I know since many years.'

I swallowed nervously. And: 'Cripes,' said Tim. 'You mean, we'll meet *him*?'

'*Aber natürlich*,' she said again.

I couldn't help remembering Gina's face when I told her I was giving the pink dress to Anna: she must have heard of this Reception somehow, and held her tongue so that I'd no time to jib. It was typical of her tough realism.

'Will – will all the top people be there?' I whispered. I thought of Himmler, Goebbels, perhaps even Streicher the Jewbaiter.

The Princess gave one of her horse-like snorts. 'Probably. There will be much jockeying for favour, you will see.'

What I did see was that protests were useless, though I made one effort: 'Please, I'd be no good at that kind of thing. I'd sooner not go, oh, please.'

'What nonsense, child. Already I am telling Winifred I bring two young English admirers of the great Richard. You will have Korbi's escort, and the Führer will barely speak with you, there will be many people eager to be noticed.' A sudden pounce in another direction: 'Yesterday you make some expedition with another student, is it not so?'

I stiffened. 'I was with three other students. Weren't you told that too, Princess?'

She was unabashed. 'Eleanor, you will do well to let older heads decide your engagements. Austria is, well, full of odd people who hold – awkward views.' I looked at her covertly. Her expression was bland. Franz had told me of her family's gift for survival; I remembered it now. Perhaps her rank allowed her areas of freedom too: the Führer must be at Wahnfried already – yet for half his visit she had been away, sponsoring a Contest elsewhere. With unwilling respect I felt that in her dowdy grandeur she could easily outlast him.

'So. You understand me, my dear child. Neither I nor Korbi would like to see your name connected with such people.' She patted my hand. She was a great patter. 'There. It needed to be said. You are a good sensible child, and you are *geboren*. Properly chaperoned you will not make mistakes again.' She banged hard on the glass partition. *'Schnell, schnell, Johannes.'*

I moved closer to Tim, who murmured, 'What does she mean, you're born? Weren't we all?'

'Our blue blood,' I answered sourly. But my thoughts were with Franz, and how he would react when he heard of the company I kept.

Franz. And we were now heading into the same stretch of country where he and I had wandered yesterday . . .

We had stood on the mountain flank, taking deep breaths of fresh air that was sharp even in summer. Gina and Peter were walking the path near the road, we could just see their heads bobbing into view now and then. Once we'd let them photograph us, arms around each other, smiling into the sun, we had given them the slip; they were perfectly happy arguing over which were the best views to take with Peter's new camera.

A faint heat mist rose off the grass. The mountain was mirrored below us in a green-glass lake. Behind us lay the high peaks guarding Franz's home town, and in the opposite direction were the forests, lakes, and stupendous castles of mad Ludwig of Bavaria. Here there was perfect peace beneath a tender blue sky.

'If only other people would let us alone! If life could always be like this. Where are you taking me, Franz?'

'A favourite place. Sometimes I come to camp there, alone.' He grasped my hand and pulled me after him up the next steep slope. On a plateau of brilliant green grass small firs were dotted, sturdily upright. Wild flowers were everywhere – gentian, orchid, rockrose, dotting the ground with colour, adding to the mountain scents.

Midway across the plateau Franz paused. 'There! And see that bit of scree? There's a cave in the rocks. I found it. I keep some things there, a week's rations too. They have never been taken. I am sure no one else knows it is there. I will show you later, Nell.'

Here where we stood we could see no further than the plateau rim. The heat thrust straight down on us, burning through my cotton dress. I kicked off my shoes, and the grass was warm as toast to my bare feet. I slid to the ground, pulling Franz down beside me. He made a sound half-way between laughter and a groan.

'Oh, Nell, don't – how can we not? Nell – '

'*Why* should we not?'

For a moment all his good intentions held, then his arms reached out for me. We lay mouth to mouth and his right hand began unbuttoning my dress.

There was no one here to spy on us, or remind us that we had no future. It was the height of happiness.

And now the Princess's black Mercedes was on the road below the same mountain, and the plateau far above was as wrapped in mist as Brünhilde's rock with fire. Down here in the luxurious car it was like gliding through smoke. Drenched tree trunks closed in on our right, too close, just as the Princess and her nephew were closing in on me, leading me into Siegfried's dragonland.

I shut my eyes and prayed fervently that something, anything, would prevent Franz from coming too.

In spite of newsreels, newspapers, and Hitler's ranting voice on radio, nothing in my calm English life had prepared me for the atmosphere in this very ordinary town of Bayreuth now the Führer himself had come to worship at the Master's shrine on the Green Hill. Everywhere were blood-red banners, coal-black swastikas, and swastika armbands; conspicuous too were the polished jackboots and the death's-head insignia of the SS. Motorbikes roared up and down the streets, ridden by young men with set faces and a look of dedication in their mad blue eyes.

'It was quiet, once,' said the old Princess. '*Kinder*, good that the villa I take each year secluded is, or we must endure all this – ' did she really say 'nonsense'?

The car swept up a side street and came to rest before a house crowned with pepperpot turrets. Korbinion's two-seater was already standing in the drive. The Princess's major domo came forward to greet her, followed by two footmen and her housekeeper. There was even bowing and curtseying and no one gave the compulsory salute. As though thought-reading the Princess said, 'All my servants have been with me many, many years. The good old-fashioned loyalty that doubtless your family enjoys, Timothy.'

Tim didn't reply, perhaps thinking of the charwomen who came and went whenever his mother could afford some help. I felt guilty at the way we were imposing on the Princess, whose attitudes in Hitlerite Germany were so ambiguous.

'The Herr Graf awaits your Highness in the drawing room,' announced the butler.

'Tell the Herr Graf we go to the octagon room. Hanni, bring tea, we are hungry and thirsty after our drive. Come, children, the little octagon is *gemütlich*.'

We followed her across a sea of patterned tiles and into an enormous room where a very longtailed Bechstein crouched in one corner. She flung off her sables and lowered her bulk into a chair. Her knuckles flashed huge diamonds, but her hands were dirty. Evidently she had a magnificent disregard for washing them, which Tim would approve.

Almost at once footmen bore in trays of food, with porcelain and sumptuous silver.

'*Ach*! A small tea after the English fashion will do us good.

So refreshing. There you are, Korbinion. Why are you not in uniform, dear boy? I like to see traditional uniforms when I am confronted by some others.'

'Aunt Greta, you will be shot if you speak like that.'

He kissed her hand and her cheek, and clicked heels before me. 'Nell.'

One of the footmen was trying to attract her attention.

'What is it, Julius?'

'If it please your Highness, Frau Wagner is on the telephone.'

The Princess extracted a muffin from a covered dish, crammed half into her mouth, and crossed the room to an antique telephone hung upon the wall. I strained my ears to understand.

'Winifred? Yes, we just arrive, half-starved . . . what?' She was chewing away, casting glances at the tea tray. 'Does he? I must be flattered, I suppose; can't one move without people reporting it, these days? . . . I joke . . . Tonight? But we only just arrive . . . Oh, very well, then. How many more creatures are you having? No, I'm not meaning to embarrass you, Winnie dear . . . I now ring off. Yes, I will bring Korbinion.' She replaced the receiver and lumbered back to us. 'How like Winifred to ignore that I have house guests, I will put that right for tomorrow. And she always acts as though people listen in, which I expect they do. I trust you will forgive, dear children, but the Führer requests my presence already at *Walküre*; there is just time, Korbi will take me – yes, Korbi, you are commanded. Go and change, or you will be shot. So, Eleanor, Timothy shall take you to see the town, and I shall arrange dinner for you both.' She poked me in the ribs. 'You need more weight. Perhaps a soufflé, game pie and a chicken with green salad – you like *pommes frites*? *Kaisersmarren* and meringues, maybe Hanni has crystallized fruits if you are hungry still, or cheese. A good white wine. You could manage on this little supper?'

'Oh no, Princess,' said Tim. 'I might wake up hungry.'

An unnerving stare. Then she gave a deep rich chuckle.

'Truth is, I'm beginning to like the old bag,' he told me later, as we strolled through the town. 'She's not quite what we thought.'

'I wouldn't like to get across her,' I said more cautiously.

'I don't mean to – too much like meeting a rhino head on, which is why I "found" your pink dress. You'll look startling in it, anyway.'

'Beast.'

'Not beast: I gave the gloves to Anna. Look at all these bloody scarlet banners, Nell – you'll clash nicely with them.'

I slept badly that night; not because of the rich supper, or my stifling and gloomy bedroom. A Führer-Reception at Wahnfried: no wonder Gina had caught her breath. To meet the top monsters was a prospect of horrifying allure. What should I say if Herr Hitler spoke to me? Certainly not *'Heil'*. Tim had been no help at all: 'I shall bow, reprovingly. Try singing the Horst Wessel Song with different words.' I felt like Siegfried approaching Fafner, except that the Hero was fearless, and I feared for Franz. If only I'd never handed over those damn tickets.

A clock struck three. Images of my father's face haunted the dark, reproaching me for visiting Bayreuth along with the élite of Nazi Germany.

At least the music would be glorious.

I slept at last, to dream of the Nibelung dwarf Alberich urging envious Hagen to vengeance on Siegfried and the gods, as he does in the last opera of the 'Ring' – 'The Twilight of the Gods'.

'Hagen, my son, hate happy people! . . . *Hörst du, Hagen, mein Sohn?*' Alberich was in shadow, but Hagen crouched there in moonlight, clutching his spear, and his face was Korbinion's.

15

'Most charming,' said the Princess. 'But where are your gloves, Eleanor? Frau Monika fails me.'

'I'm afraid Tim must have missed them.'

'You shall have a pair of mine, and carry them. You approve the dress, Korbi?'

'It is unusual. We do not lose her in the crush, eh?' Korbinion's face quivered; as he offered me his arm his left eyelid drooped into a wink.

'She's representing our national emblem, you see,' explained Tim, following the three of us across the hall. '"But oh, the fairest flower that in the garden gro-ows,"' he crooned, '"the fairest queen it is, I ween, the perfect English ro-ose".'

I kicked backward and caught him on the ankle.

Outside Wahnfried there were motorbikes everywhere and uniformed guards. Korbinion was considerably saluted. We were conducted into the house, where a tall, striking and distracted-looking woman fell on the Princess's neck.

'Greta, how late! Wolf has been asking for you, he is out in the garden already, circulating.' She spoke in German, but I got the meaning.

'A charming frock, Winifred. Now here are my young people. Korbinion you already know – '

'Küss die Hand, gnädige Frau.'

'And these are my English guests, Eleanor and Timothy.'

Two brisk nods disposed of us. Frau Wagner took the

Princess's arm and hustled her – if such a word could be used for that majestic waddle – through the house and out into the grounds. We followed.

'"Wolf"?' I hissed at Tim. 'Who's he?'

'Dunno. Sounds dangerous, though.'

Korbinion had overheard. 'Wolf is what Frau Wagner's family call the Führer. Wolf, or Onkel Wolf.'

'Goodness. She must be on terms.'

'And a pretty suitable name, I should imagine,' muttered Tim.

He was taller than I expected; more noticeable and full of bonhomie, joking with his entourage. The caricatured moustache bristled strikingly, and the eyes were really alarming, deep blue, hypnotic. Near him I felt drawn into something strong and strange and dark. It wasn't just the surrounding kow-towing to supreme power, it was some kind of seductive life (or death) force. When he turned to us crying, *'Die Fürstin!'* and advanced to seize her hands and kiss her warmly on each cheek his charm was undeniable. Silly insignificant man, I told myself firmly – and couldn't tear my eyes away.

Korbinion received a hearty welcome. Then the Princess beckoned me and Tim, though I tried to hide behind his back. Questions through an interpreter brought Tim's shy admittance of soon entering the Navy – the first I'd heard of it. The Führer beamed, slapped him on the shoulder – *'Ein ganzer Kerl!'* – then moved on to me, who stood shaking and crimson in my pink dress. To my immense surprise he bowed and kissed my hand, and it seemed that in return I was expected to kiss his cheek like a favourite niece. In my bemused state I heard him say something about the bond between England and Germany.

Photographers were present, cameras clicked. A not-quite-fatherly arm was clenched around my waist. Locked to the Führer's side I was drawn willy-nilly about the grounds while before my glazed eyes faces of the famous and infamous appeared. Some people were joked with, even introduced: *'Unser Herr Doktor – '* (Goebbels) – *'und mein treuer Freund, der Herr General Feld Marschall'*. (Goering's vast figure in a white uniform starred with medals.) The possessive grip was cuddling me like a new teddybear, as Korbinion stalked behind us, and some way off Tim stood staring, pop-eyed.

I had said, 'I won't be their pretty pink doll', but here I was. A bit of pretty propaganda too, another petted Englishwoman simply dotty about Adolf. Suppose Franz saw a newspaper. But he would know it wasn't my fault – wouldn't he? Then another chilling thought: if his father saw one . . .

At last Frau Wagner herself released me, trailing some celebrities for presentation.

'Auf wiedersehen, mein schönes Kind.'

I went reeling across the lawn to Tim's side.

'That's right, Nell, always aim high. He's unmarried, too; think he's a good match?'

'Don't bitch, Tim. Get me away from those newsmen, fast.'

'Darling Nell, you can't cry here, and there's no escape, not in that dress.' Tim gave my arm a shake and handed me his handkerchief. 'Blow. And remember Tommy's training for performances, because here comes Korbinion.'

'Well, child, you had success.' The Princess's shrewd eyes examined my face. 'Too great, perhaps, although Korbi does not see it so, men can be stupid. And dear Winifred is furious: she must rearrange her seating plan so that you and I and Korbi – and our young sea cadet – may sit close to the Führer in his box tomorrow. Wolf!' she added. 'Such nonsense, and wolves always gobble people in the end. No, Korbi, not hush in mine own house. Ah, coffee. Pour our dear Eleanor a good strong cup.'

After the Führer's attentions, Korbinion seemed even more

eager for my company. The Princess encouraged him, and I begged Tim to stick closer than a brother.

'I'll try. Bet she's got other plans, though.' He was right. She expected him to dance attendance, while Korbinion guided me around Bayreuth as if he were a walking Baedeker.

'Everyone stares so,' I complained, as we crossed the main street.

'In England, I remember, that is not correct. Here, of course, we have nothing to hide.' He wasn't without sly humour sometimes.

'I said stare, not look at.'

'But naturally. Word goes round: Wolf's *schönes englisches Mädchen.*'

'For God's sake,' I said indignantly, 'that stupid unimportant scene?'

'Unimportant? Aha, the jealous whisperings, here in *Valhal*!'

'Your darling Führer was simply playing to the gallery.'

'Hush, Nell. Many Germans speak English, as I do.'

'You're not all that taken with him, are you?'

'He is my country's Leader,' Korbinion said smoothly. 'Please, behave. And he admires the English – you too, my Nell.' He held my arm in a possessive grip. I knew that I should never breathe freely till I was sure Franz had thought better of running such a gauntlet. It was almost a relief to see Irma and her friend Heinrich approaching, but I was soon regretting it. They had evidently seen the local papers.

'How lucky your friend is not with you, yesterday, when you the Führer meet. *Ihr Freund* Franz,' she added, with a sly glance at my companion.

'Franz? Ah, I remember.' He affected vagueness. 'The angry young student, still wet behind the ears?'

'Sehr sympathisch, der Freund Franz,' bubbled Irma. *'Schade,* that he also a – '

'Oh, look, Korbinion,' I interrupted her quickly, 'isn't that the shop where your aunt said I might find souvenirs for my family? Come on, let's go and see.'

'Heil Hitler,' yapped Irma. Her arm shot up like a puppet's.
'Heil Hitler,' responded Korbinion.
'Goodbye, Irma.' I almost dragged him away.

'Nell, I must speak to you; quick, before lunch. We went to call on Winnie W. On the way we ran into Franz.'

'Oh, Tim!' My legs wobbled. I sat down hastily. 'I did hope he'd think again. There can't be another Jew anywhere in Bayreuth – not with all these beasts wearing death's-heads knocking about the streets.'

'You're wrong, actually. The Princess says Winnie makes Wolfkin protect Jewish artists, mostly singers.'

'So she may: celebrities, sometimes, but not Jews in general, you idiot. Did you speak to Franz?'

'We had a few words together. He says he must see you. He gave me his address: some flat shared with another student, the Innsbruck sponsors fixed it for the ticket-holders. Oh, cheer up, Nell! If he's any sense he'll lie as low as a mouse in owl-country. Lunch, Princess? Great. I'm ravening again.'

After lunch, while the others drank coffee, I murmured an excuse and escaped from the villa wearing dark glasses and carrying my guide to Bayreuth. I found the flat quite easily, and luckily Franz himself opened the door. I dropped guide and glasses and went straight into his arms.

'Nell,' he said, after a brief though satisfying pause. 'Why were you in disguise?' He pulled me down on to the sofa. 'Do not shiver so.'

'Oh, Franz, my darling – they're all there – the top beasts. She – the Princess – took us to Wahnfried. And I've met some – even him – I couldn't help – ' My voice came out muffled against his chest.

'I heard. And there are also pictures. Do not let them use you, *Liebling*. Come back to Austria with me now, today. Don't go back there.' He stroked my hair.

'If only I could but . . . how can I walk out on Tim, or the Princess? She's got us all in at the deep end. We're – ' I swallowed – 'to – to sit with *him* tonight.'

There was silence. Franz's mouth was set in a bitter line, making him seem much older, drained.

'Don't look like that, Franz, please. It will all end in two days – and then home – to Innsbruck.'

'It will never end, unless you come with me now. I promise, Nell. You do not understand these people, you are too – too simple. Too clear, I mean: crystal . . . like water.'

But I'd fallen into deep muddy waters through not thinking straight nor fast enough. Now I should have taken the limelit path of escape and cut and run; I knew that really, yet worrying about Tim and Gina, Tommy and the Princess, confused me. Against my intuition I said, 'Truly, I can cope, if we don't lose our heads. *Please* go back yourself, Franz, I'll manage everything all right. We'll be together then for my finals. In Innsbruck. Free.'

'Leave you alone! Here? And we never shall be free.'

'I must go now,' I said desperately. 'Please, Franz, do try to understand. I got myself into this, somehow I'll get through; if I have to plead illness, I will.'

He gave way, and kissed me. But then he said, 'There is the fascinating Graf, I suppose.'

Even now I can't bear to remember the row that followed. It was as bad as only first quarrels can be. That we made it up before I left was some comfort, though not enough. As I walked away from the house a car drew out and passed me slowly, driven by an SS man. I blinked my tear-blurred eyes and wondered whether I'd seen or imagined a second figure seated in the back.

16

'So! My aunt says you are ill, and cannot come tonight? All the way from Innsbruck to hear Wagner, and then this sudden illness? You do not look unwell.'

Korbinion's hands were heavy on my shoulders.

'I am unwell. See how flushed I am – Tim thinks so, anyway.'

'Cousinly concern? Now hear me, *Liebling*: certainly you will come, otherwise you make it awkward for my aunt, and for myself. Here in Germany there are times when it is impossible to say "no". You will behave graciously, *geboren* as you are.'

'Your aunt wouldn't force me to.'

'No, she would not: *she* is *geboren*.'

'Korbinion, I had better say a quiet goodbye and go back to Innsbruck.'

'Fit enough to travel? Though not well enough to accept the Führer's own invitation?' He swung me round to face the window. The car that had passed me near Franz's flat was parked outside, the SS man still sat at the wheel.

'Stay, Nell. It will be best for all your friends. Besides, you and Tim will enjoy the performance.' He laughed and bent to kiss me. I drew away.

'*Mein Schatz*, perhaps you do not know yourself. You could have scraped out of coming here, had you really wanted to, mmm? Now you are here, you will behave.'

'You don't tell me what to do.' I began to walk towards the door, but he followed and seized me by the waist. His face was sullen and stubborn as a thwarted child's, the brutality in his voice was not a child's.

'You are not in England now. You will do exactly as you're told. Look out of that window, and think again – ' he dropped his voice to a more ordinary tone – 'and do not be so obstinate, my sweet Nell – kiss me.'

I glowered when he released me, and he smiled as though it thoroughly amused him. 'And do not tell my aunt too many lies – Why, here she is. Nell feels she can manage to come with us tonight.'

'Korbi has changed your mind for you, I see. He will look after you, like the good boy he is.'

'Indeed, our delightful Nell may be sure of that.' Before his aunt's approving eye he kissed my hand.

The night was fine and hot as we drove up the Green Hill to the opera house. Among the people walking there I saw no sign of Franz. The number of uniforms was conspicuous, and I thought gloomily what a strong race they looked, how naturally warlike. Korbinion wouldn't leave me alone. His vanity was so extreme that he couldn't believe in my reluctance, or else he enjoyed it.

The atmosphere in the foyer was almost hysterical, the combination of the Führer and *Siegfried* had produced something like religious fervour. There were crowds of women wearing full frumpish evening dress and expressions full of soul.

We waited too. Even the Princess wasn't bold enough to arrive there after the Führer. When he came there was a tremendous surging forward, with cries of '*Heil Hitler*' going off like firecrackers. I clutched at Tim, murmuring, 'Keep together.'

'If Wolfkin lets us.'

Winifred W. and some little Wagners in full fig were trailing after *Onkel*; the famous face was a mere foot or two away, sulky this time, something must have annoyed him. I was relieved that he barely seemed to notice me, before we were hustled by some aide in the great man's wake.

Once the performance started, I managed to lose myself quite often in its sheer magic; until something would jerk me back from the fantasy world where Siegfried the hero forged Nothung, his dragon-slaying sword, and the dragon theme itself growled on the tubas, and I would realize again that I was sitting in my privileged seat close to the prize monster of the century, who was cosily surrounded by Wagner's descendants and, less cosily, the Party élite; while somewhere within these same wooden walls sat my dear love, whose own existence was threatened by the magnetic Leader's. '*Tod an den Juden!*' I felt sick.

My hand groped for Tim's, and held it. If only I could leave Bayreuth tomorrow! How right Franz had been, but it was too late now. To go near his flat again was to invite the attention of the SS. The dreadful visit must run its course. Whatever his aunt might think, Korbinion's intentions weren't serious: he certainly didn't believe Tim's lies, so he was just enjoying power games. How far would those games take him? In crazy Nazi Germany they might start turning real. I remembered my father's misgivings with despair.

The Wagner tubas were grunting loudly away.

'Bear up, Nell,' whispered Tim. I squeezed his hand. Should I avoid Franz, if I caught sight of him? Or should I try to find him during the first interval?

Korbinion saw to it that I had no chance. He hovered sharp-eyed at my elbow, partnered me solicitously to supper in the nearby restaurant, and then said with sinister sweetness, 'Now come and charm Wolf again, *mein Schätzlein*.'

'Please, no. I can't talk to him.'

'But he loves modest *Mädchen* – very alluring.'

At least the photographers were absent. Korbinion's self-confident manner achieved a pathway for us through the Führer-circle. The sulks had gone: the blue eyes held a wild exalted swimminess. I was delivered up, received the same embarrassing favour as yesterday, and was invited to spend the last act of the opera at his side. After that even the fight in the second act, when Fafner the dragon lumbers out to defend his possession of the Ring, failed to distract me; even Furtwängler's conducting of the Woodbird scene, when Siegfried is guided towards sleeping Brünhilde in her circle of fire, left me cold.

During the next interval the Wagner party was besieged by important people. Instead of returning to the restaurant Tim and I and Korbinion went strolling in the grounds. Tim started an argument with Korbinion about the rival singers' merits, which gave me a chance to trail a little way behind them, searching the shifting crowd for a sight of Franz; at last I saw him, alone and rather lost-looking, staring at the ground. I felt a surge of relief.

Suddenly, as though his eyes were drawn to me, he looked in my direction. He smiled happily as I began pushing my way towards him.

A hand seized my arm from behind. Tim's voice said, 'Where are you off to, Nell? I wouldn't get lost in this crowd, if I were you.'

He was right, of course. Franz was probably dying to confront Korbinion, although even my proud Franz might think twice about the danger of intruding on the Führer's circle, considering the presence of so many toughs who looked as if they wouldn't know one note of music from another.

The crowd pattern had shifted again, and Franz was already lost to view. Sadly I followed Tim and there, straight ahead of us, were Irma and Heinrich, centre of some animated friends. I saw brownshirts among them and stopped short, but Irma had already seen me. She dragged Heinrich in our direction.

'El-ean-or! Teem – *und der Herr Graf*! Shall we now back to the *Festspielhaus* together walk?' She must have known where we were sitting, we were so prominently placed.

Korbinion's expression was freezing. He said very

distinctly, in German: 'Nell! Please to remember whose guest you are tonight. It is not permitted to encourage outsiders without direct invitation.' Of course it was true, although just then we weren't near the main attraction, and he needn't have said 'outsiders'. Several people turned to stare.

Not even Alberich's expression when he cursed the gods could have bettered Irma's. Her clear little voice dripped treacle: '*Aber*, El-ean-or, where hides *der Freund Franz, der Jude ist*, while you with the beloved Führer sit?' She turned away.

I looked at the ground. Korbinion's voice sounded almost indulgent. 'So? That angry young fire-eater of yours is a Jew? He has courage, to come here on your tickets.'

'Franz is not a Jew,' I lied. 'That's Irma's spite.'

'Really? She would make deliberate trouble for you? But why?'

Tim came to my rescue. 'Oh, because she lost her semi-final and thinks Nell won for the wrong reason. Knowing the Princess, I mean. And then, to see us with the – er – beloved Leader, must have truly got her goat.'

'Goat?'

'Made her angry.'

'Goat! What a saying. Well, our *Schätzlein* does not concern herself with such low and unpleasant things tonight.'

Schätzlein. All on a par with that pink dress. I gave him a weak smile, and his hand caressed the small of my back. Grovelling could soon become second nature to me in this atmosphere of hidden threat. Korbinion was looking flushed and triumphant, and I made a mental note not to be left alone with him later that night – I had hysterical visions of myself seeking refuge under the Princess's bed.

'The interval is almost over, Tim,' Korbinion was saying. 'Take Nell to the Führer's box, whatever happens she must not keep him waiting. I will rejoin you, but first I have a duty.' He disappeared into the crowd.

'Don't worry, Nell, gone to find a girl-friend, I expect. Bet our Korbi has one in every town, unknown to the Princess. Come on, back to be *gefressen* by Wolfkin.'

'Korbinion wouldn't believe Irma, would he? Anyway, surely he wouldn't want any trouble near his Führer?'

'Forget it, Nell.' Tim sounded impatient. 'I'm sure Korbi always keeps his bread butter side up. Try to forget about Count Drac altogether, pretend you're having the evening of your life. One more day to go, then we're home and dry.'

Home and dry seemed a long way off while I was forced to sit through the final act at the side of Germany's most loved and hated figure. Now and then the magnetic voice muttered something in my ear, as the lovers clung together beyond the flames to passionate music from the Master's hand. The love duet ended at last. Tears were streaming down the Führer's face while a frenzy of applause almost rocked the opera house. Wagner – the old sorcerer as Franz called him – had again acted like possession on his devotees.

'Wunderbar, mein Kind,' sighed the Führer, wiping his forehead repeatedly. *'Wunderbar, diese Musik.'*

Thankful to escape at last into the fresh night air, I stood apart with Tim, watching Herr Hitler and Frau Wagner submerged in a sea of worshippers. When they moved towards the waiting cars the Princess came looking for us.

'We will walk home, children, since Wagner is so – Korbi, find Johannes and tell him to take the car ahead. Eleanor, you go with Korbi, perhaps?'

'I'll come with you,' I said decidedly.

'We will all wait for him,' decreed the Princess. Even she seemed depleted by the evening, and perhaps the company. If I could believe my ears, and my German, she was murmuring, 'What my dear Albrecht would have thought, such terrible people.'

The crowd, held back till the departure of their Head of State, now surged out and around us. Covertly I watched for Franz.

'The sound was specially good, wasn't it?' said Tim. 'Fantastic acoustics.'

'Wonderful . . . I'll never want to hear Wagner again.'

'Oh, come on – you never will with Wolfkin.'

'Associations, though.' If only I could just catch sight of Franz for one moment, reassure him with a look, before Korbinion – now intercepted by friends – rejoined us. Oh Franz, *hurry*.

Instead it was Irma and Heinrich who came out arm in arm, giggling as though they shared an amusing secret. The audience was thinning fast.

'What *is* going on?' said Tim suddenly, at the same moment as the Princess exclaimed: 'How very strange! Children, one would think there was a fire!' For the crowd had turned and begun surging in the opposite direction. People were running about distractedly, and others pressed back behind us towards the entrance. There was no longer a hum of appreciation but a different sound, ugly, snarling, cruel, that rose from the crowd like the hunting cry of an animal:

'Jude . . . Jude . . . Jude.'

'Oh, my sweet God, it's never – '

'Now steady, Nell.' Tim held me back, as a knot of struggling men spilled out of the entrance in an explosion of violence. I broke from his grip and ran towards them, for Franz was there, outnumbered five to one, but punching and kicking with the recklessness of despair. He was defiant and streaming blood, and around him was a circle of distorted, hating faces, a nightmare vision straight from hell.

'Franz – *Franz!*'

Holding up my flowing white skirts I forced my way between the onlookers, who were behaving like people at a bullfight. In my ears rang that jeering cry of *'Jude, Jude'*.

'Nell!' Tim forged after me. 'Eleanor!' shrilled the Princess. Someone else cried out loudly about insults to the Führer from the Jews.

One of my shoes came off, I stumbled, shoved a fat woman from my path and hammered on the back of a tall man barring my way. He moved aside. The space ahead was clear, where Franz now lay spreadeagled and being kicked. His face was livid, his lips were drawn back in moans of pain and fury. I flung myself towards him, sobbing out, 'Oh, Franz – '

One of his attackers turned to face me, laughing. Rage surged, and I struck him in the face. With one expert, almost contemptuous, flick of the wrist he flung me aside, so that I went sprawling and lay gasping and half winded on the ground. When I raised my head Franz was limp and motionless, with shut eyes. Someone sniggered and drove a boot into his side. Together his assailants lifted him on to their shoulders in a parody of Siegfried's funeral march.

'Franz?' I whimpered.

He managed to open his eyes, recognized me, and tried to smile. I was pulling myself dizzily to my knees when someone or something crashed into me, catching me a crack on the head.

I slid into darkness with Tim's frantic voice echoing in my ears, 'Nell, Nell . . . ' Korbinion's mingled with it, shouting orders. Then the darkness was black as Hagen's night, shot through with pain.

17

Hours later, I surfaced to true night. Lamplight shone on a strange room smelling of disinfectant. My thoughts wouldn't hold. They drifted away from me like clouds, though sometimes I was conscious that someone, somewhere, was in dreadful need. Why wouldn't things make sense, whose was the danger? It was too much effort to remember. My head ached furiously. I moaned. A white-veiled woman leaned over me murmuring, '*Schlafen, schlafen.*'

When I woke next it was broad daylight. Pain stabbed through my left arm as I raised myself in bed, aching all over, but my memory had cleared. How long had I been lying here while Franz . . . where was he, was he even still alive?

I tried to struggle out of bed but my legs wouldn't obey me, they felt heavy. Suddenly panic almost ousted fear for Franz. Tim, the Princess, even Korbinion – why had they left me here alone and helpless in this high and narrow hospital room? With its one small window it was like a prison cell, except for the flowers everywhere: on the table, the washstand, the bedside locker. There was no bell within reach. I called and called. My voice was feeble, but at last a nurse heard me and came running. She was followed by a young doctor, with cropped hair and steel-rimmed glasses. Tight-lipped with discretion, he was adept at ignoring my badly-phrased questions.

After his visit the *Schwester* in charge came to settle me more comfortably, wrapping a shawl around me in spite of the heat. A square card decorated the opulent roses by my bed, and she handed it to me with a beaming smile. The signature danced before my eyes.

A midday meal was brought me. I hardly touched it, although I knew all my strength would be needed to help myself and Franz, if that was possible. My legs were still useless, and still nobody, not even the *Schwester*, would tell me anything.

Tim came to see me an hour later, nervously sidling round the door. His mouth was grim, he looked older since I'd seen him last.

My voice was almost my own again: 'Oh Tim, thank God you're here! What have they done to Franz? Where is he? This beastly place is a nightmare, no one tells me anything and my legs have gone flop.' I gave a sob. 'For God's sake, Tim, what's happened to Franz? Do you *know*? Is he – They didn't – kill him?'

Tim sat down gingerly on my bed. 'Steady. Franz isn't dead, he's in the lock-up, I dug that out of Korbinion. People do survive beatings up, however bad. Don't go to pieces, Nell, or they'll throw me out. I'm only allowed a few minutes.'

'I'm not going to pieces. You'd feel lousy half-paralysed. It's terrible here, they treat me as if I'm half-way between an idol and a prisoner. And look – ' I thrust the square card at him.

'Lord! Roses from Wolfkin himself? No wonder you've got nervous shock. That's what's wrong with your legs, they've told us. You'll be fine as soon as it wears off.'

'Oh, my God.' I wiped my sweating face. 'I'll go mad, Tim, unless I know Franz is really all right, and safe.'

'I don't suppose he is, but they wouldn't kill him, Nell, he's Austrian. More public scandal? Not here at the Festival. No one but us – I and Korbi and now the Princess – knew you were bent on rescuing a friend, they just thought you'd blown your nut, not being used to such scenes. But the spotlight's really on you now – our Korbi says you've had another write-up in the press. Wolf's English pet.' Seeing my appalled expression Tim added, 'I don't suppose Franz will see the papers.'

I winced. 'I must talk to the Princess.'

'Ah, well, I think she's playing a bit hard-to-get. I have to tell you, Nell, I've made a clean breast.'

'Now, of all moments?' I began to chew the end of the shawl.

Tim reached over and removed it. 'Hey, don't swallow that. It seemed best, what with the publicity looming.'

'I suppose so. Was she furious?'

'At first. But the old girl's got her own grim sense of humour. I made it plain it was all my fault, my great love of Wagner, and you got stuck with our noble ancestry.'

'That was noble of you, Tim, anyway.'

'Mainly true. Apart from that, she's in a delicate position, poor old bag; Franz coming from her very own Festival. For all her *geboren*ness, she doesn't want to be *gefressen* by Wolfkin either.'

'Tommy!' I said suddenly. 'Does she know?'

'Only that you're in hospital, after a fall. Don't worry, she won't leave the brats to Ruddigore, but she's sent for your Dad. He's coming tomorrow afternoon.'

I fell back against the pillows. 'Oh, thank God.'

'Don't cry, Nell.' Tim looked uncomfortable.

'I'm not crying . . . I'm quite desperate to think what we can do for Franz.'

'We?' Tim sounded alarmed. '*We* can't. You might sweet-talk Korbi into helping when he comes.'

'Him? He won't come, anyway, not if the Princess won't. And I'm sure he caused it all,' I said with loathing. 'What about that sudden call to duty just after Irma spilled the beans?'

'You can't be sure. It could have been darling Irma herself. You keep on his right side if you can, Nell, I'm sure he's a beast if he's crossed.' Tim grimaced.

The door opened.

'All right, *Schwester*.' Wearing an exalted zombie look Tim sketched a '*Heil*' towards the flowers. She beamed on us both.

'Wait, Tim! You're not still going to "Twilight of the Gods"?'

'I wanted to call it off since you can't, and poor old Franz is – But the Princess thinks it's best.'

'Oh. Don't you get *gefressen*.'

'Not me. And she's right, you know. Guess what sort of a wise old bird she is? A mugwump – keeps its mug on one side of the fence and its wump on the other. Glad to see you can still laugh, Nell.' He was gone.

To my amazement Korbinion arrived not long afterward, calm and smiling as if nothing had happened. I lowered my eyes, not to show my feelings. He bent over me, and I shrugged the shawl close around me so that he couldn't kiss my hand.

'This hot day and you are cold, Nell?' He sat down, looking at the flowers.

'They're from Herr Hitler.' Surely he and the Princess must know, or he would never have come.

'I left mine with *Schwester*. Some from my aunt too. She sends her regrets that she cannot come again today.' (I liked that 'again'.) 'The opera starts early and she was commanded to Wahnfried. Now she will see you tomorrow. You are well looked after?'

'Very. I think – Herr Hitler's flowers, you know?'

He smiled. 'And Tim has been to see you.'

'An hour ago.'

Duelling was something I should have to learn as we went along. He's dying to talk of yesterday too, I thought, so let him start first. And I prayed: Let me know what to answer. Please. I waited for an opening.

'Fräulein Armstrong was upset to hear of your – mishap. She seems to blame herself. She sends for your father.'

'So Tim told me. It was hardly her fault I – fell.'

Silence.

Then Korbinion laughed. 'Discreet Nell. Fell? You would do very well over here, even though you're not *geboren*. I wonder, would your father let you stay?'

I looked at him narrowly and decided it was all part of the power tease. He couldn't really want it, certainly not after yesterday. So I smiled and said nothing. He changed his tactics: 'Nell, do you not trust me? You need protection from some things.'

'I have it, haven't I?' I said, glancing at the roses. 'And why shouldn't I trust you? Thanks for bringing me flowers, and do thank the Princess too. She's kind, specially when I think how we tricked her. Tim never deceived you, did he?'

He raised his eyebrows. 'So I gave myself away.' A falsely sentimental sigh. 'Perhaps I just wished you to stay, dear Nell.' Then he pounced: 'So! What of this Franz, then?'

I moistened my lips. 'I told him it was mad to come.'

'And yet gave him your tickets? Not very friendly! Strange.'

I'd hate this man to interrogate me, I thought. But that's just what he's trying to do. He can't care two damns about me. That doesn't make him less dangerous, though. He's so vain, he's upset that I prefer a Jewish student.

'He – he's just a music student, like me,' I stammered. 'He wanted them s-so badly.'

'And you could deny him nothing? That is more like love.' He raised a hand. 'No, don't deny *that, liebes Kind!* The way you went storming to his rescue – charming.' He didn't sound charmed.

'I can't bear to see bullying,' I said faintly. Sensation was returning to my legs; they shook.

'You will get battered if you rush into every street fight.'

'We don't seem to have them much in England. And it wasn't a street.'

'The beautiful dress, ruined. What a pity! And you, my sweet child, I can only say we were horrified.'

'It was most awkward for you.'

'Luckily you were, well, not unobserved exactly, but thought hysterical. Perhaps imagining silly things after an emotional evening? You were worried that your young cousin Timothy could be attacked . . . the Führer himself was distressed to hear you believed such things would happen in our dear Fatherland. So, all ends happily.' His gaze was bland, slightly malicious. He was looking at his watch.

I sat up poker-straight. 'I don't know if Tim's heard this surprising version. But nothing "ends happily" with my – our friend Franz beaten up for being half-Jewish and dragged off – where?'

'Didn't you deny that he was Jewish? Never mind. Forget him, *lieb* Nell. I daresay he will be returned to Austria some day when his crime is expiated. Chastened, I hope, and aware of his lowly place in life.'

'Expiated! Crime! What crime?'

'You are so English, *mein Schatz*. Jews do not attend performances attended by the Führer.'

'No one could have known Franz was one, except – *You* went off on some sudden "duty" after Irma spoke.'

'*Kind*, I acted to prevent further – indiscretion. One little call to Innsbruck, and I knew young Franz's pedigree. Anyway, once the girl Irma and her friend began spreading rumours about him anything could have happened.'

'Anything did. And his "indiscretion" would have gone unnoticed till you had him beaten up.'

'I resent that,' Korbinion interrupted coldly. 'I acted as I thought best. I did not specify a beating, sometimes it is hard to stop things getting out of hand. He was unwise not to submit meekly to public expulsion. The beating followed his refusal to salute the Führer's portrait.'

'Acting for the best is your forte, isn't it?' I flashed, remembering the fiery swastika.

'Nell, to quarrel will only make you ill. Rest now, so that you can travel to England with your father. Perhaps I will visit you there one day.'

'Travel to *England*?' What chance would I ever have of seeing Franz again, even if they released him? 'But I'm – I'm in the Innsbruck finals.'

'It is arranged.' Again he looked at his watch.

'I can't go back to England yet, I can't even walk.' Weakness made me tearful.

'And you think yourself fit for the finals, when you are hysterical?' He stood up, wearing a triumphant look. '*Schwester* does not forgive me if I upset you, so calm yourself. *Auf wiedersehen* till tomorrow, when my aunt accompanies me. Oh, do you know, I almost forgot? There is a surprise, a great honour for you. Our beloved Führer leaves tomorrow for Berchtesgaden, and intends visiting you first. A recompense for what you suffered, I believe. About eleven.'

I stared at him in horror. 'No. A thousand times no.'

'*Sei nicht so dumm, mein Herz*. You wish to make more trouble for my aunt? Doubtless you are overcome by the honour done you. The Führer was charmed to hear of your success, and your choice of "*Heidenröslein*" for the finals. Sad you may not sing it at Innsbruck, instead you shall sing a verse to him. Photographers will be present to provide some pretty souvenirs.'

My hands clenched beneath the shawl. 'I'd sooner die. I – I shall lose my voice.'

He scowled. For a second something uneasy showed through the urbanity; could it possibly be fear? I felt a flicker of hope. 'And suppose I say or do the wrong thing,' I murmured. 'That would be dreadful for you, Graf Korbinion.'

'Why should you? What idiocy! What sort of thing?' he said sharply.

'I just might imagine that you knew about Franz all along, because I told you in Innsbruck, don't you remember? And you said no one would ever guess he was a Jew. Although of course when Irma started talking you had to act. If I specially asked the Führer, don't you think he'd release Franz? I mean, if he knew that Franz was your protégé – and your aunt's?'

Korbinion's look of victory had been wiped away. It was replaced by the air of an experienced duellist caught napping by a pupil.

'So if I could see Franz, before he was sent safely home – Why, nightingales wouldn't match me.'

'It – it is out of the question to see this Franz. It would be . . . known,' said Korbinion.

I just looked at him.

'It is possible he could very quietly be released. Afterwards.'

'No, now. Today. And I want proof that he's not badly hurt.'

'Nell, be sensible, please.'

'I am very sensible. Everything's done by mirrors here. Most of the truth must be known already, through the Gestapo. All right: I'll join the act: *"Heidenröslein"*. Pretty pictures of a doting *Mädchen*. There's a price.'

'That boy cannot be released today, there are formalities. But if I discreetly see he is looked after, and that he leaves tomorrow for the border, by lunchtime, you will behave?'

I hesitated. 'I must have proof.'

'What proof can I give you?' he asked helplessly. '*I* am not SS. That Corporal was seconded as my driver, a watchdog, perhaps. Mine is an old proud Corps to which my father and grandfather belonged. Will you not trust my word?'

Trust, when I had defeated him? Although it was a draw, really; there was still that hateful bargain.

'How bad is Franz?' I asked bluntly at last. 'Tim's bound to hear anyway, at Innsbruck.'

'Ribs cracked, teeth broken.' Korbinion shrugged. 'He is not too bad, one bruises if one is beaten. Believe me, Nell, he was lucky to be Austrian. He got off lightly, you would say.'

'If anything worse happens to him I shall – shall write all about it for our papers when I get home. The whole truth.'

'So, my dear, you are no *kleines Mädchen* after all.' A half-smile, even tinged with respect.

'And you'll personally see he's all right, straight away?' I insisted.

A curt nod. Certainly I hadn't underestimated his influence. 'He will go by train, with escort.'

'Tim can go on the same one, then.'

'Impossible they should travel together! My aunt takes Tim by car.'

I shook my head. 'Oh no, it must be the same train. Tim would do that, for me. I'm sure someone guarded goes in the van or a special compartment. Once they reach Austria Tim's free to see him anyway. Oh – and I want to see Tim before he goes.'

Korbinion hesitated.

'The English papers would simply lap up this story.'

Korbinion rose. There was no handkissing, just a formal salute. 'Very well. Tim shall be here early to see you. *Mein Gott*, I hope we never fight the British.'

He had reached the door when I added, 'Please, would you ask the *Schwester* for writing paper and a pen. I must write something for Tim to take Miss Armstrong.'

Another curt nod. Korbinion didn't believe me but he didn't quibble.

'Be discreet, please. I shall be here tomorrow for the Führer's visit. *Heil Hitler!*' It was the first time he'd barked out that salute at me. I shut my eyes.

'Goodbye, *Herr Graf*.'

Some while later the *Schwester* brought me pen and paper. She clucked over my tearstained face, and brought me wine as well.

'Franz, *mein Geliebter . . .* ' But it was an impossible letter to write. I began it a hundred different ways, and each seemed false and formal when I remembered the green valley of the Inn, our solitude on the mountain, the brief joys and glory of our meetings.

18

'Hate leaving you all alone in dragonland. How are the legs?' asked Tim.

'Better, thank God. I only needed someone's arm to the bathroom.'

'Your Dad will be here this afternoon, anyway. Got any messages for Gina?'

'Tell her she might have warned me about that Reception. And that I wish I was coming back. And both of you try to make Franz understand if he ever gets to hear about me singing "*Heidenröslein*" – though it's all in my letter to him. You will see he gets it? Certain sure?'

Tim patted his breast-pocket. 'Safe with uncle. We'll do our best, Nell.' He looked less than his usual self, pale in his formal concert suit. 'I could tell him you were blackmailed.'

'If you get the chance. He's so – proud.'

'Do my best,' Tim repeated. 'Can't promise more, can I? Get well, Nellie.'

We both started at the sound of military footsteps in the corridor and a distant rattle of '*Heil*'. Tim backed towards the door. 'I'll be lurking,' he whispered. 'But we won't get more chat together, you should see what's lining up outside to greet your little friend. Don't bite Wolfkin or we'll never cross the frontier.'

The German press made much of the compassionate arrival with fatherly look. The satellites and hangers-on crowded behind the Führer into my slip of a room. The hypnotic eyes and dab of a moustache confronted me from the end of my bed.

The Princess was there too, massive in grey silk, her friendliness tinged with reproof. She stationed herself well apart from *Reichspressechef* Dietrich, Dr. Goebbels, and – horror of horrors – Streicher the Jewbaiter. The Führer's adjutant, Brückner, clicked heels at my bedside and presented me with a second bouquet of roses on his master's behalf. Like a puppet I sat upright, clutching the freshly-picked flowers, whose thorns pricked me, whose stems dripped water, while the haunting and bitter irony of Schubert's song flowed from my lips, as smoothly and effortlessly as though I'd been hypnotized

> *Sah ein Knab' ein Röslein steh'n,*
> *Röslein auf der Heide –*

Tommy herself would have been proud of my performance.

Then more photographs were taken: of the Führer himself clasping my shoulder while he murmured emotionally, *'Das englisches Röslein'*; of the Princess and Korbinion; of music loving Goebbels – and lastly of Streicher seizing both my hands, which I tried to prevent too late. Flash, click. Recorded forever, before the jokes and laughter, and presentation of a gift.

Afterwards, to my acute embarrassment, the Führer slyly suggested that Korbinion might like to offer me a permanent home in Germany. The Princess looked out of the window as though her thoughts were far, far away, and the warmth of Korbinion's response didn't ring quite true. Then at last it was over. They had all gone, even Tim who would shortly be leaving for the station, and the military footfalls and distant *heil*ing faded into silence.

I was left alone, staring at the Führer's gift: a signed photograph of himself, framed in silver, inlaid with his initials and small gold swastikas, and surmounted by an eagle. I turned it face downward with a vicious slam, and sobbed myself to sleep.

When I woke, my father was sitting by my bed.

'Daddy!'

His expression was very grave, and he shook his head at me reproachfully. It was the only reproof he ever gave me, the only sign of how he felt about this shame I had brought on everyone through ignoring his advice.

To be home again in safe green England was like living in a dream. I drifted through the days, willing myself to believe that all was well with me and Franz, surely at some deep level a love untouched and untouchable by brutal circumstances must survive. At other times I knew, bleakly, that everything was over.

Soon Tommy and the others would be returning home. Once she rang to ask after me, and again when the choir came second in the finals, but there was no word from Franz, or Tim and Gina. Several times I tried to ring the *Gasthof* myself, always without success. Either the lines were booked, or my friends unavailable. Once I managed to get through to Gina, but no sooner had I said, 'G., have you heard from Franz?' than the line went dead. After that I even tried to ring Franz at his father's address, though unsure if I remembered it correctly. Directory enquiries gave me a number, and the phone rang and rang the other end, but there was never a reply.

The choir returned home two days after their successful finals. I knew they might be delayed, and after dinner went upstairs to my room and tried to listen to the wireless. It wasn't long before my father called out, 'Nell, have you gone to bed already? Tim and Gina are here.'

I switched off my set and rushed along the landing.

'Tim! Gina! Come on up!'

They followed me to my room. Gina sat down in silence on my bed, twisting her hands together. I looked at her, and she looked away.

'Well, you are a nice pair,' I said at last, 'you might have kept in touch.' My voice came out thin and small, I felt I might shatter if anybody touched me. Neither of them spoke and after a moment Tim came to join me by the window. The twilight made everything look fragile and unreal, it silvered the overblown roses whose petals were already falling in the summer heat.

'Did you give Franz my letter?' I asked Tim at last.

'When we reached the frontier. The guards left him then. I saw them go and went along to the compartment.'

'Yes – ?'

'He seemed – miles away, somehow. They'd tidied him up a bit, but they couldn't hide the bruises. His mouth was terribly swollen. He was white as – as – Just terrible. He didn't seem to want me there.

'Perhaps I should have waited, not given him your letter then. Waited till we were both back at Innsbruck . . .' Tim was making heavy weather of it. 'But he didn't show up for the finals, not even with his choir.'

'Tim, don't keep me on tenterhooks.'

'No . . . you see, the guards had got hold of an early paper. I saw it there, turned back at your picture. You and Wolf. You and Streicher. I begged him to read your letter. When he wouldn't I said it explained everything, you'd probably saved his life, told him what you'd done for him – but I couldn't get through to him at all. He wouldn't listen. It was like talking to someone stone-deaf, or – dead.'

I swallowed. 'Did – did he say nothing? Not even how he felt? About me?'

'When I told him none of it was your fault, he looked quite blank. Sort of, past feeling anything. He said – Oh Nell, do you really want to hear?'

'No. Yes. Every word. Come on, Tim. I know it's hard.'

'She's easily swayed, he said. I knew, when she said she was going, she truly wanted to. She deceived me before, just small things, but – so she could again. I thought what we had was real but we – we are poles apart. *Mein Gott* – even to speak with Streicher.'

'Didn't he – read – the letter?' I said dully.

'Nell, he – he tore it into little bits, and threw them from the window. Then he said, Get out, Tim. Leave me. And turned his back. There was nothing I could do then, so I went away.'

There was an awful tearing sensation in my chest. I had this dreadful pain inside like a bleeding wound. I'll die of it, I thought. I hugged myself hard, wrapping my arms around myself, but the tearing pain went on, moving up into my throat.

'When he reached Innsbruck Tim told me all about it, Nell,' said Gina awkwardly. 'I felt so much of it was my fault, I did push you so about Bayreuth. When Franz didn't turn up again we got his address from Peter and went to his home to try and see him. It was shut up, for sale. He and his father had gone away. Oh Nell, I'm sorry! Is there anything we can possibly do?'

I shook my head, still staring at the roses.

After a while Tim and Gina went away, silent and subdued. I barely noticed their departure. I wasn't seeing the roses, only my torn-up letter scattered like snow from a speeding train.

Weeks afterwards I did hear from Franz, in a manner of speaking. He sent me his translation of '*Liebst du um Schönheit*'. There was no letter or address, and try as I would I couldn't read the postmark.

In faint pencil he had altered the third verse:

> If you love Nazis,
> O never love me!
> Love the Führer,
> He has such charming ways!

I sat looking at it a very long time, it was like watching a black mist roll over the landscape where we had been so happy. What could I make of the fact that he had left in the last verse? I could only remember how young he was as well, how hurt. I wrote to him once more at his school, care of his choirmaster, but I never heard from him again.

1965

19

All this, at least the bare sad outlines of it, Clare gently though remorselessly extracted from me on my first evening in France. My plane landed late at Nice, and I was pleased and surprised to find her waiting for me at the airport.

'Maestro let me come to meet you, he made one of the others lend me a car. It's quite a drive. Is this all your baggage, Nell?' She went ahead of me and stowed my case in the back of a Renault.

'This is nice of you – and of him,' I told her, as we swept up the bends of the Corniche.

Clare turned to give me a brief smile. She was sunburned already, it gave her a gilded look. 'Not *so* nice. I want to talk.'

'About the boyfriend? Clare, not so fast!' A furious truck driver was shaking his fist at us.

'Sorry, wasn't thinking. Yes – about Toby. Or more about you, really. I am having trouble, you see.' She frowned at the driving-mirror.

'Goldfinch trouble, as Laura would say?'

'Well, not how you'd think, exactly. It's another girl, parents from the West Indies, like his. Her name's Delilah, and it suits her! She and Toby have always been very close.'

'She writes to him?'

'Worse, she's here. She's a musician too – brilliant.'

After a moment she added shyly, 'Nell, what did Laura mean about you? Would you really tell me?'

'You want me to tell you now?' I felt lazily reluctant to spoil my first day of escape from the office.

'Yes, now. You've an hour or two at least,' said Clare relentlessly.

So I told her, in fits and starts, between moments of teeth-gritting terror since Clare had only passed her driving test three months before. At least she displayed a flair for avoiding disaster.

'Poor Nell,' she said at last, when I had done. 'How truly horrible. *Never* again?'

I shook my head. For some while we drove in a silence broken only by the blasting of truck drivers' horns. Then Clare said, 'Can't think why Laura thought your story might put me off Toby, it's not at all the same. I'd say the real message is, "'ware other people interfering". Makes you think, doesn't it? Delilah would try, all right. And if *you* hadn't allowed them to – ' She broke off.

'Manipulate me? Yes.' After all the years the bitterness was still there, not even very deeply buried.

Darkness was falling. I stared up at the star-sprinkled skies, so much clearer than those of England.

'Here we are,' Clare said abruptly, as she turned the car off the road, into a short driveway. 'Your hotel's just up here, it's got marvellous views. Can't come in, Nell, I must return the car. Thanks for telling me all that, you didn't really want to, I know. But there's so much else I want to ask – did you never try to find out what happened later?'

'Yes, after the war. But there's not time to tell you now,' I said thankfully, as the car drew up outside the hotel.

'That's all right, I'll come and breakfast with you, shall I? You can tell me then. And I'll get Toby to join us a bit later for coffee, so you can meet him. Seven-thirty wouldn't be too early, would it? I've got an orchestra rehearsal after nine. Maestro's an early bird.'

'*Dear* Clare,' I said, kissing her goodnight. 'And I thought I was here on holiday!'

Next morning we breakfasted together on the hotel terrace

which, as Clare had said, provided panoramic views of the Alpes Maritimes. She barely allowed me to finish one croissant before fixing me with a remorseless eye.

'Come on, Nell! I do really want to know what happened.' Then she softened slightly. 'If you don't mind, that is.'

I poured myself more coffee, and took another croissant.

'It's all right. It's far away and long ago.'

' "After the war", you said. You couldn't go back to Austria earlier?'

'Oh no. In 1938 things got so bad in Europe, my father wouldn't let me go abroad. Then afterwards – I was going to marry Ned, you see. But I had to know first about Franz. Don't misunderstand me, Clare. I loved Ned a good deal, it hit me hard when he died, some years back. Because he was a fighter pilot he had a hard war, wounded, burned. And I was nursing, that was how we met. It seemed a worse waste of life not to marry someone I could help, you know, and have children.'

'But you didn't have them, that's sad too.'

'Sad . . . yes.' I paused a moment, then continued: 'After we married, Ned and I used his gratuity to start up the Agency. I was through with singing – I expect you know all that from Laura, anyway.'

'But tell about the search for Franz.'

'Gina and I went to Vienna after the war. We worked for the International Red Cross, which was tracing displaced people. It gave me my chance to search the records. Piece by piece I got the whole story. They'd left Innsbruck, Franz and his father, directly after what happened at Bayreuth. The house was sold, before it could be taken from them, and they went to live with cousins, nearer Salzburg. After the *Anschluss* the Gestapo soon came for them. In the night, of course. Franz's father was taken straight to Dachau, where he died.

'But Franz – he'd been out that night with friends. Neighbours saw the van and guards waiting, and got a warning to him. They told him his father had been taken. They gave him food and money enough to go into hiding for a while. Then he reappeared, down and out, looking for work in Innsbruck, trying to find someone who'd help him escape. Too late, of course.' I traced a pattern on the tablecloth. 'Herr Schmidt, his old choirmaster, helped him secretly for a bit. It was Schmidt who told the authorities all this, later. In the end Franz was caught, and sent as slave labour to a German factory. After three years he got ill.' I swallowed. 'After that, the camps. Just one of the millions blotted out.'

'Oh, Nell! Was that certain?'

I nodded. 'All the names were checked. When I knew for sure I – I went home, and married Ned.'

'And you felt able to?' Clare looked at me disapprovingly. 'After that?'

'My God, Clare, you've no idea what the general state of things was then! So many people's lives wrecked. Tim killed on convoy duty, after all his jokes about the Navy – I often think of that. And Dan's health wrecked – he was a prisoner of war. I just felt Ned and I must *build* something. Ned at least was happy.'

'Sorry,' said Clare, rather embarrassed.

I stared at the mountains. So long ago . . . and peaceful mountains still shining in the sun. With an effort I said lightly, 'Now tell more about Toby and this girl called – what did you say? Delilah?'

'Funny, it was through her sister that I met him and she's as nice as Delilah's nasty and can't tell one note from another, and I only wish Delilah couldn't.' Her expression changed to one of pathetic eagerness. She was looking over my shoulder. 'We can't go on talking, Nell – here he is.'

Toby was walking towards us with a loping, graceful and arrogant stride. His long crinkly hair floated in the breeze, his unbuttoned shirt, open to the midriff, revealed a powerful throat and chest. He sat down opposite me without a word, putting an arm around Clare.

'Nell Hathaway, my aunt. Nell, Toby.'

'Hullo,' I said, to that inimical glare.

He nodded. Just.

'You can relax, Toby. Nell doesn't think you're a goldfinch.'

'Holy Moses, man, we've the great understander here, huh?'

'He doesn't usually send himself up like this,' Clare assured me.

'I'm relieved,' I said coldly.

'You'd sooner I was white,' he challenged me. 'Say it, then. Don't let's have the usual hypocrisy.'

'White, black, coffee – I'd sooner you made Clare happy. Each time you kiss, that chip on your shoulder must surely get in her way.'

Clare laughed. And I added, 'Your teeth are whiter than hers at least, a great comfort to my hypocritical heart.'

Then we were all laughing together in an eased atmosphere. The tension went out of Toby's shoulders; he released Clare, and looked much younger, and said rather shyly, 'Could I have a coffee?'

The order was given.

'Toby plays guitar, 'cello, clarinet *and* writes mod. jazz,' Clare told me lyrically, while we waited.

'An all-round musician, then. How enviable. Is it the 'cello or clarinet for this orchestra?'

Another rather shy look at Clare. 'Fournier's giving Master Classes for 'cello here. I may get the chance to play the Saint-Saëns when we tour.'

'A super start. Such a public pat on the back from Maestro could open most doors.'

Toby nodded, sitting back in the sun and closing his eyes against it. Even when he was motionless and silent the power of his personality was plain.

I saw Clare stiffen suddenly, wondered why, and turned my head to see a girl walking towards us with a dancer's swaying step. She was dramatically dressed in black and scarlet. With that cloud of bronze-black hair and magnificent carriage she could have been Spanish, if her skin hadn't been twice as dark as Toby's. I thought she looked pugnacious, and as if her name suited her very well. She was watching Toby with a hungry, possessive look, timelessly older than her youthful face.

Clare glanced at me and I saw the fear behind her eyes.

The newcomer approached our table. 'Toby.'

His face was immobile. His eyes stayed shut, his long body swayed slightly to and fro.

'Delly?'

'I've been looking for you, then someone told me you were here. We had an early session planned together. You forgot?'

Clare and I mightn't have existed.

'Toby and I are having coffee with my aunt,' said Clare. She sounded unsure of herself and Delilah easily ignored her.

'Toby?'

'Later, honey. You know Maestro's called an orchestra rehearsal.' Toby gave her a full warm golden smile. He reached out casually to hold Clare's hand. Defensively, I thought. Yet there had been that smile. And the air was positively sizzling with Delilah's vibes. I thought it was time to take action.

'Won't you introduce us, Toby?'

'Yah, well, this is Delly, an' we've known each other since we was kids. And Mrs. Hathaway's Clare's aunt.'

'Sit down and have a coffee, if there's still time. I didn't know families or friends accompanied the students.' In my voice an echo of the Princess's, so long ago.

Delilah hesitated before sitting, turning her shoulder to me. 'No, not coffee. Toby – '

'They don't, but Delly plays tenor sax and trumpet like she was Satchmo'.'

'It must have been a bond,' I said.

Delilah gave me the benefit of her dark and sizzling gaze. 'It's not the only one. All Toby's ancestors and mine were slaves,' she declared passionately, and with such drama that I could almost see the ring around her neck.

I didn't accept the challenge in her voice. Instead, I leaned across the table to offer her a croissant. 'Wouldn't you like some late breakfast? Toby, do order your friend some coffee, it's no day for remembering ugly things.'

To my surprise Delilah subsided, drooping a little, and murmured, nothing to eat, thanks, but she'd like a fruit juice.

Toby gave the order, and began questioning me about my rôle at the Summer School.

'Part holiday, part talent-spotting,' I told him, watching Delilah from the corner of my eye. She glowed. So she was ambitious, too.

'Come and sit in on one of our sessions, Mrs. Hathaway. Toby's written a short piece for tenor sax, guitar and drums that really wows you. I'm his saxophonist.'

'And she's great,' said Toby.

'I'm sure she is. Tell me when.' I took out my diary.

'When, Toby?'

He grunted. 'Not today . . . there's things to change. C'n we let you know?'

I nodded. 'I'm here all this week, sunning myself and drowning in music. Are you in on these sessions, Clare?'

'Sometimes I go along to write things down for Toby.'

'But not often,' said Delilah. 'There's no real need.'

'Sure there's need. There's always need.' Toby put his arm around Clare and pulled her to his side. 'She's my l'il old inspiration.'

The smile Clare gave him was like a sunburst.

Delilah scowled. 'It puts me off, having other people there.'

'Girl, it would take the Bomb to do that,' said Toby. 'And it won't put you off to have Mrs. Hathaway, she has one gorgeous show of an international agency, isn't that right?'

'I'm glad Clare gives me such a write-up.'

'You could lend an ear to the quartet I'm playing with,' said Clare. 'That's Maestro's way of setting up groups for individual coaching by visiting grandees.'

'And a real fine 'cellist she is, too. Aren't you, honey?'

Again, that sunburst smile.

'I know that already,' I said. 'She only needs more confidence to be well away. How do you get on with Maestro, Clare?'

'You don't get on with him, you react – like to natural forces! If he wants to, he gets on with you. And then he's a love, suddenly. So kind.'

'And so attractive,' I added.

'Luckily Clare's eyes and thoughts are all elsewhere.' Toby gave her thin shoulders a giant hug. Delilah looked away. She said nothing, but I could sense powerful emotion and was glad her fingers, fidgeting with a teaspoon, didn't hold a knife.

The three of them went off together at last, late for the orchestra call and expecting a skinning from Maestro Strogani.

Poor Clare, I thought, watching them go. Plainly Toby's in love with her now, *but* – And Laura's opposition would pale beside Delilah's, and I could imagine the female weapons that might be used. I closed my eyes, feeling the touch of mountain sunlight gild my face. Life is all moments. You cannot take on other people's problems. Sadness passes, love remains. Perhaps. Footsteps again on the terrace. I opened my eyes and for a moment thought myself crazy: Franz was walking towards me. The bright world took a dizzying swoop, sun motes were swirling together into mist. I put both hands palm downward on the table to steady myself, and looked up when the world ceased rocking. It was a young face looking down on me. Now I could see how young, though I was hardly to be blamed for that moment's madness, the likeness to Franz was there, if not so much as I'd first thought. It was caused perhaps by a trick of light and shadow on middle-European features.

'You are Mrs. Hathaway?' Careful English, a pronounced

accent either Austrian or German. Again, the old twist of the knife.

'Yes, that's my name.' I was recovering slowly.

He smiled. 'Clare I meet just now, outside here, on the road. You are her aunt, yes? She says I may introduce myself. But forgive me, please. I am thinking you are unwell?'

'Just a touch of the sun,' I said, trying for lightness. 'Or the height here, the air.'

'The mountains. You must take it slowly, yes?' He sat down opposite me. 'I am Johannes Spengler, a violinist. Leader of Clare's *quatuor*. She says you will hear us? From us four then, I am inviting you.'

'Fine. But she forgot to tell me when.'

I took out my diary again, ashamed of my shakiness and stupid disappointment when he said his name. 'By the way, shouldn't you be with the orchestra now?'

'Yes, I should be there to listen, though today Maestro reduce the strings.' He gave me the quartet's practice times, and stood up, glancing at his watch. I longed to delay him because of that elusive likeness.

'Come later this afternoon, we play Mozart,' he tempted me.

'My mouth waters. I'll come.'

He gave me a little bow, which reminded me vividly of Franz handing me the bouquet at Innsbruck station. Dear God . . . perhaps Mozart would be unbearable after all. The aching sorrow. The sweet gaiety.

When he had gone I sat on alone, aware of feeling chilled, as though cold wind and cool skies had blotted out the sunshine. I thought of Franz's death, and Ned's, and of how the jealousy and infighting and planning at the Agency were now my life. Pointless, it seemed. And it could have been so different. But self-pity never got anyone anywhere. There were worse tragedies than mine. Some people never found anyone they could love, or had handicapped children. And I might never have achieved anything in life at all, after such an unhappy start. Now it was more fitting to be troubled for Clare.

20

Local families had thrown open their doors to the visiting students of the Summer School, and Clare herself was lodged in a rambling farmhouse; in its living room, under an eminent violinist's eyes, the Mozart Master Class was held. As I listened attentively to Clare's playing I realized that worry was affecting her form. How much easier her path would be if she could fall for someone less magnetic than Toby! Or do such comfortable paths really exist?

Johannes was a substantial asset to the quartet, one could tell that right away. When the second movement began I shifted my seat in order to watch his face: Franz as he might have been, born into a happier time – joy in doing something supremely well, faith in the future. I saw him shoot an inquiring glance at their tutor after a difficult passage, and get an approving nod. After a time, when discussion was in progress, I crept away.

Two days later I drank coffee with Maestro Strogani on the terrace of his hotel. As usual a bunch of budding musicians were waiting like ravenous puppies to devour his words. This time he waved them aside, with a laugh.

'I and the Signora have serious business to discuss.'

'Not serious! This is really my holiday.'

He waved that aside too. 'Holiday? I know the Signora! Which of my budding geniuses do you pursue? Or is it perhaps myself?'

'Why not? We're always ready to take on new clients.'

Maestro was firmly entrenched with a rival firm, but he

took my suggestion in the spirit in which it was made. 'Ah, when my agent dies – he threatens I bring on the heart attack – I come to you, it is a promise.'

'I'll book my cardiac surgeon right away. Before that exciting day, though, Maestro, tell me about your own favourites here?'

'I, favourites?' He feigned astonishment. 'Still, I could mention a girl from Sweden – over there, with the blonde hair. A superb woodwind player.'

'I picked her out at the rehearsal last night.'

'Ah, trust the Signora's ear. And from your misty land?'

'Can I push my own niece's claims? And Toby Cyrus impresses me, he's such a personality. And composes already.'

'Signora, you read my thoughts. He bursts with talent, that one; crackles like the firework. He involves himself with the little Clare, yes?' Strogani loved a good gossip, his ears picked it up as easily as music. 'I do not underestimate her talent: there is force, there is something special to be challenged. Poor girl, she lacks confidence at present, hmmm? Love must not affect one's playing.'

'Perhaps that's easier for a man.'

He looked outraged. 'It is never easier. For music, life must be dedication. Me, I dedicate.'

'You're so right. I wasn't dedicated enough. There's also young Johannes Spengler,' I added hastily, seeing that gossip-loving ear bent in my direction. 'I've heard him lead his quartet.'

The bright old eyes softened. 'You name my other eaglet. Strange, music comes where it wills. Johannes' family tend the vines. Perhaps he throws backward, you would say.'

I hid a smile. One did not correct Maestro's English.

'Do you know all your students' backgrounds? That's quite a task.'

'Aha, at the interview I am good: I probe. The family history – that too is important. The young Clare worries me, a little. *Molto bella* but delicate, no?'

'No. Laura – my sister – is as strong as an ox, Clare's father too.'

'Excellent, then the little Clare is the racehorse type. Health is important.'

'Johannes has a good healthy background, anyway,' I said. 'Vines! So long as they don't lead to drink.'

Strogani shook his head at my flippancy. 'His mother dies a few years ago – tubercular, poor woman. There were of course the war years, when it was not good to be young in central Europe. So, perhaps he has not the weakness in the genes. His talent is great, and no one forces him to tend the vines – a wonder! Yet he is a good boy, not spoiled.'

'I should like to help him in his career,' I said. For Franz's memory – and for my own sake – I felt an urge to help Johannes. A sort of repayment for the havoc I had caused. 'He reminds me of someone I once knew, who was as unlucky as Johannes is fortunate. It's a strange difference, to be young now. With your permission, I'll speak to him.'

'D'accordo, Signora. Now I must to my orchestral *bambini* and belabour them; and here comes the little Clare, to find you. No sympathy, Signora, I implore. One stiffens the spine, yes? *Va bene, Chiara mia*? Love improves the playing? If not, I forbid!'

'Va bene, Maestro.' Clare gave him a starry-eyed look, and the moment his venerable back was turned changed it to a hideous grimace. 'Old demon. Laura needn't have worried. He's worse than she is, for different reasons.'

I laughed. 'He's just begged me to stiffen your spine.'

She drooped. 'Oh, God. All my disks have slipped. It's awful, Nell. It's Delilah. She's on at Toby all the time. She's more anti all of us than Laura's anti Toby. She *uses* it to prop up sex. Perhaps I should have Toby's child.' She sat down and gazed at me so defiantly that I guessed one wrong word could decide her.

'My poor Clare. Would that get you anywhere – and the child?'

She gave a sad sniff. 'She's so dramatic. She makes me feel bloodless and – and inhibited.'

In honesty I could offer her little comfort. I almost quoted Gina's words of so long ago: there seems no future in it. But they hadn't stopped me.

'It depends a lot on Toby,' I temporized. 'I see his fascination – call it what you like, he's magnetic. A charming personality. He'll attract people as a honeysuckle attracts bees. But I hardly know him, and you do – is he a stayer? That's largely temperament. Some people – not always the worst, either – can be pushed off course by any little breeze.' I didn't add that Toby's vitality combined with his age made it likely that he'd wander. Faithfulness wasn't in fashion. Even dominant and possessive Delilah would find him hard to hold.

'Delilah's not a little breeze, she's a tornado.' When I was silent Clare added rather resentfully, 'I suppose you'll say you could tell that your precious Franz was a stayer, though you didn't have much time together, did you? Anyway, you were both Europeans – and if that sounds like Laura, it's not. Only – ' She paused, lost for words.

'We're all a little bit of our distant ancestors and their ways, as well as ourselves. I understand.'

She looked at me gratefully. 'Toby's ancestors might have expected me to set up in one hut with our kids, and Delilah in another with hers – and we'd both hoe our patches and sleep with him in turns.'

'Like top people in eighteenth-century England, in fact except that someone else would have hoed the patches! Honestly, Clare, all I can advise is: concentrate your efforts on what's strong and real between you and Toby. Don't get your thoughts stuck on Delilah and defeat; you'll simply hypnotize yourself into failure. You're important to Toby now, he's made that plain enough.'

I looked at my watch.

'And if you're late once more for orchestra rehearsal Maestro will have the skin off your spine.'

Clare didn't confide in me again; what free time she had was given to Toby. I was glad of it; the last thing she'd want, or need, would be an Agony Aunt breathing down her neck. Outwardly there was little to show how things were going between them. Sometimes I met them wandering off towards the rehearsal rooms, and once with Delilah, all three of them talking and laughing like the greatest of friends. More often they were absorbed into a bunch of students under Strogani's steely though beneficent eye.

In the orchestra's rare moments of freedom I was mainly in Maestro's company or his eminent friends'; or I sat apart, studying my talent-spotting notes – although I'd been small help to Clare, my time hadn't been wasted. At the first chance I waylaid Johannes and told him I'd be happy to handle and advise on his career once he felt ready for a larger stage.

'You are too kind, Mrs. Hathaway. But, you understand, I would speak first with my father – and with – '

'Maestro, perhaps? He does know I'm suggesting it. I know you want to be sure you're in the right hands. Talk about it to Maestro yourself.'

'In the past my father acts as my manager, when he is not busy with the vines. I have given local concerts, you understand. If I were not musician I would grow things, like my father. He says: after so much destruction, it is a good life.'

'I like the sound of him. Yes, you must talk to him too. Tell him we've very strong contacts, worldwide. I can safely say we're as good at launching newcomers as anyone else – and very much better than some.'

Johannes was still looking doubtful when he left me, and I was almost regretting my offer. This Summer School hadn't been all joy. The problems of Clare and Toby; Johannes' fleeting likeness to Franz in a smile, an intonation – something of all this was like a pattern repeated though out of true. If I could have seen Clare less troubled I would have been glad to leave.

A day or so later I sat in on an ambitious Stockhausen rehearsal. It was very hot, and at midday Maestro called a break for coffee. Johannes slipped into the seat beside me.

'*Ein Kaffee*, Mrs. Hathaway?'

'Oh – thanks.' I took the cup. 'How do you like playing Stockhausen? I confess he's my blind spot.'

'What is that?' He looked puzzled. His English was so good that explanations weren't usually needed.

'He doesn't wow me, as Delilah would say.'

Johannes laughed. 'For the mind, he stimulates. Like a bathe in ice-cold water.'

'Clare finds that too?'

'Yes. She is very accomplished, you know. Only – '

'Lacks confidence, as Maestro says.'

'This is a pity, I like her so very much. We have become friends, you see. Do you take her on your books too, Mrs. Hathaway?'

'Oh, no. Not my own niece. If she makes music her life I'll recommend her to a management just starting. The directors are all young, their drive and enthusiasm will help her find her own feet.'

He nodded, earnestly. 'Mrs. Hathaway, I am so very – flattered, you choose me.'

'Ah,' I said, amused. 'So you *have* talked to Strogani.'

He reddened. 'Forgive me, I did not realize – quite how grand – '

'Forget it. Now tell me instead, since you're her age, is it in music or herself that Clare lacks confidence?'

'Herself,' he answered at once. 'That gives rise to the other, no?'

'Toby Cyrus, in fact.'

'More Delilah than Toby, I think. Toby is *sympathisch*, but blind in some things.'

'She reminds me of "Carmen",' I said. 'Headstrong, violent and flamingly attractive. And pugnacious!'

'Clare too is attractive. It is more subtle, though.' His

detachment made it plain that the most he felt for her was friendly concern. I thought it a pity; he wouldn't overwhelm her, as Toby did.

Johannes saw Maestro returning to the rostrum, and stood up. 'When do you leave, Mrs. Hathaway?'

'The day after tomorrow. I'm glad you're here, Clare may need friends. I'm lying low now, that's plainly how she wants it.'

'If I can help, I will,' he promised. 'Thank you again, for saying you'll help me later on.'

During the Summer School the whole orchestra gathered for meals in a converted barn. On my last morning Maestro met me walking up the village street, and pounced on me like a vigorous and charismatic eagle.

'Aha, some assignation, yes? For no other reason do you escape to be alone, one can be sure.'

'Certainly, Maestro. Didn't you see one of your flautists is missing?'

'Impossible to shame the Signora.' He seized my arm and pressed it lovingly against him. 'Now you do not escape lunch at my own table.'

'There's nothing I like better than lunch with you – a treat of the grandest sort.'

'Flattery, hah? You are not Eve, but the serpent. I would have you know I am past sixty years old.'

'None of those poor babies will be safe for another thirty years at least.'

Laughing together, arm in arm, we entered the barn. He looked round him with a commanding eye. 'Who shall join us at our centre table? Our eaglets? Perhaps the little Delilah also – a type straight from opera, no?'

Beckoning to his chosen few, he disposed us so that I was on his right, Clare on his left; and Toby, Delilah, the favoured Swedish girl and Johannes completed the circle. I felt we were puppets in the hands of a master puppeteer, who loved to get those sensitive fingers into every pie.

'Well – ' his glance swept the room – 'here we are, at the end of our first week together, still far from what we shall achieve, and already the Signora tires of us and departs. So, Signora, now look into that crystal you keep hidden in your pocket and tell us who, at this table today, will have the greatest future?'

'You should tell us that, Maestro.'

'No, no – I am just a performer with the bâton, an old beaten tired-out hack. It is you who watch and know.'

'Mmm, yes . . . ' I looked down into my wineglass. 'Here is one for whom I see a great and unusual future. A bright particular star.'

'Ahhhh – ' theatrical sigh – 'Hear this, children? So! Who is the lucky one upon whom the Eye falls?'

'You, Maestro.'

He roared with pleasure. 'Did I not say it was impossible to shame you, Signora Serpent? Now, my infants, here is excellent veal, and wine. Eat, and be strong. You will need it, when I get my hands on you.'

After the meal, when he had pushed his chair back and was lighting a cigar, his eyes flicked round the table with sharp amusement in their depths, as well as challenge. 'And now – ' he raised his voice so that it carried across the room – 'what of the concertos, eh? For instance, the Saint-Saëns?'

The eagle-glance swept the room, and there was an expectant silence. All eyes had swivelled towards him. Old play-actor, I thought, though with respect.

'Raw you may be, my children, but I tell you now, I am not altogether displeased with you.' A deep chuckle. 'No, not altogether. When we tour I have already my soloists in mind – soon all shall be made clear; though, let me assure you, it is as great an honour to be elected to this orchestra and to play with it, as to be the soloists.'

Nobody believed him. They were all as ambitious as their age, their talent, and their individuality allowed. I could sense ears pricked, and breaths held. Only Toby seemed totally relaxed. Was he so sure of the outcome, or more philosophical than I would have thought? Then I noticed the way his hand gripped his wineglass. Both Delilah and Clare were watching him as well – Clare with too much heart in her face, and Delilah with the smouldering expression that should have been ridiculous, but wasn't. I saw her glance from Toby to Clare, to Maestro and back again to Toby.

Having stirred the wasps' nest Maestro blew a cloud of smoke towards the ceiling, and added, 'Some of you may consider applying for a grant to help you with your further studies; perhaps even at the Berkshire Music Center in Massachusetts, where they have the Tanglewood Festival, you understand? And I shall be watching you with that in mind. Work hard, children, and remember it.'

You old demon, I thought: that's increased their tension, all right – though perhaps you know what you're about, people whose nerves won't take the strain are no use in this profession.

'Well,' Maestro was saying, 'and how would you enjoy Tanglewood, eh, my little Chiara?' He took his cigar from his mouth, drew Clare to him, and kissed her on the ear. She looked staggered and so did Toby, and again Delilah watched them all with that long considering stare.

I said my goodbyes after lunch. Maestro kissed me on both cheeks. '*Ciao*, Signora. Until the autumn, yes? You come to my concerts at the Festival Hall?'

'I'm looking forward to them. *Ciao*, Maestro.'

Then I kissed Clare and Toby, and was surprised by the warmth of Delilah's farewell till I remembered the Agency.

Johannes came with me to the door. 'I too shall see you in London, perhaps soon, Mrs. Hathaway?'

'I hope so. Keep in touch when you've sorted things out at home. And, Johannes, could you – would you – '

'Mother Clare?' he said, grinning. '*Natürlich*! How else would I keep in your good books?'

21

After the Summer School I went on to stay with friends who owned a villa near Florence, a dreamlike place in which to idle away the time. The return to my London working life was hard, and Clare's problems were eclipsed as I wrestled with musicians' temperaments and my own. There was no word from Laura; and none from Clare, which I hoped was a good sign, meaning she was well and happy. Then one late September evening I reached home to find her waiting outside my door.

'Clare! Why didn't you phone me at the office? Have you been waiting long?'

'Oh – not long. I've meant to come and see you for ages, Nell.' She followed me inside, and stood staring vaguely into space. I saw she was thinner than ever, and hollow-cheeked.

'Sit down, Clare. Would you like something to drink, on this horrible cold evening? Wine?'

'Please, Nell.'

I busied myself with glasses. 'Here you are, then. And eat some biscuits too, you're looking famished.'

She gave a faint smile. 'I haven't eaten much just lately. I did hope I looked dramatic, not famished! Laura keeps saying so, anyway. And that she's lost her little girl.'

'Laura would.'

Clare sipped her drink, and then said suddenly, 'It's finished between me and Toby, Nell. All over.'

'I'm so sorry, Clare,' I said, meaning it. 'How sad for you. I thought he was a charmer, though none too easy. Are you certain? One can sometimes be mistaken.'

She shook her head. 'No, I'm sure. Nothing left. It was all ruined, and I – I wasn't clever. I walked straight into it.' Her control crumbled, she began to cry. 'It's been awful since. Oh God, it hurts,' she said, between her fingers.

I let her cry for some while, then I put an arm around her thin shoulders. 'Tell me. If you really want to.'

She scrubbed at her eyes like a child. 'I do. It's been hell not talking to anyone . . . I kept going crazily over it, thinking I could have changed things if I'd been wiser out there.'

I knew all about that, from experience.

'After you left, everything went well for a while, we were really happy together. Such tremendous happiness. Even Delilah seemed to slip into the background. You know, Nell, Maestro's interest – I think that sort of pushed Toby into seeing me differently himself.' She gave a wry grin.

'Well it might. Strogani's a famous connoisseur. To have caught his eye, even temporarily, is some feat.'

'It gave me a boost too.' She looked at me sideways. 'Odd, wasn't it? I mean, he must be a hundred.'

'Don't be silly, he's a vigorous sixty-four. Anyhow, men like the Maestro are a natural law in themselves. Power and experience and personality are magnetic.'

'You can say that again. I think it's partly why I feel so awful about Toby, he's going to be like that. He's not better than other people exactly, he's – more than other people. I'm dreadfully sure I'll never feel so intensely about anyone again, not in my whole life.'

I might have repeated 'Don't be silly' if the most intense moments of my own life hadn't taken place when I was her age.

'It was all so marvellous for just those few days. Somehow Toby and I, it was – it felt – '

'Unassailable?'

'That's the word. It was so right – you know? I just didn't believe anything could come between us, ever.'

I knew all about that feeling too.

'But it came the last way I'd expected it. Nell – ' she was screwing her damp handkerchief into a ball – 'would you ever have believed Toby could be crazily jealous?'

'Most people can when they're in love. There's a fine difference between that state and being loving! But you're not telling me that because Maestro – '

'Oh no. Or at least not like that. Only Maestro did say that if I applied for a grant to help me with studies in America he'd be happy to recommend me. And he said it publicly. It was all that devil Delilah's doing. I might have known she hadn't given up, she was too quiet. I was a fool.'

'Clare, my dear, I cannot believe that Maestro takes Delilah's advice.'

She actually laughed. 'Not that, no. But she wasn't afraid of him – in awe of him, I mean, like most of us were. And she – she kind of wormed up to him. And one day, after Fournier left, she told Maestro she was just wild about the way I played the Saint-Saëns concerto, better than du Pré – she'd heard me play part of it when I was helping Toby. I know this, because Johannes overheard her.' She swallowed. 'Maestro sent for me and had me play it through, and he said I should be the soloist on tour. It was fantastic in a way, though it was *awful* – because things weren't right with me and Toby after that, it wasn't the same, I could feel him resenting me and trying not to – '

'But didn't he resent Delilah saying that more?'

'Can you believe it, he's convinced she spoke without thinking – and how lovely and generous it was of her when I'd shown how I disliked her!'

She paused, twisting her handkerchief, then continued.

'I went to Maestro and tried to ooze out of it; of course he knew why. But he was furious, he said I could either accept his decisions or pack and go home. So Toby had to swallow it with a good grace and I think he really tried, but – Anyway, two nights before the tour ended there was a farewell party for Maestro, sort of thank-you from us all, and he chose that night to praise me before everyone – said I'd been his ugly duckling that was now a swan, and he went on about the Berkshire Music Center and Tanglewood again. Lots of other people loathed me, besides Toby! It's funny, Nell, I'd have liked to play badly if it made things better for us, but when it came to it, I couldn't. You must think me so weak.'

'My dear Clare! You've got a will of your own (luckily, when I think of Laura) but it's nothing to Maestro Strogani's.'

She gave a sad smile. 'Thanks. You make me feel slightly better. Anyway, Toby went back to his room with Delilah that night, not me. And next day we had a horrible row. And he blurted out that it couldn't have worked for long, and that she helped his work and I'd be in opposition to it. And that if we'd had a child later it would have suffered! Oh God, it was just like Laura, I wouldn't have believed it . . . But do you know what I keep thinking, Nell? Wish I hadn't taken the pill. Were – were you ever sorry you didn't have Franz's child?'

'Yes,' I said honestly. 'Though not then, I was too miserable.'

'But later on? And you've regretted it all your life,' said Clare shrewdly. 'And if it still hurts, after all that time, you'll understand what I'm feeling now.' Her expression was bleak. I couldn't think how to comfort her.

'Toby's a bit young to be a father,' I said lightly. 'And a baby just now would ruin your chance of a career. Maestro's no fool, he thinks very highly of you. Could you have suppressed your talents to help Toby's? Could you have lived with that heavy sort of jealousy? Your gift's outstanding. It will bring you into touch with fantastic people. Just give it time.'

'Like your mother told you? Oh darling Nell, never mind.' She hugged me suddenly. 'But do you know what Toby said? That if I really tried to get a grant to help me as Maestro suggested, he'd wait another year before he tried for one himself.' She got up abruptly and crossed to the window, pulling aside the curtain to stare out into the rainy dark.

'He wouldn't be so bitter if he weren't so young and desperately ambitious,' I said gently. 'It's a tough mix.' And, when she didn't answer, 'You will apply?'

'Yes. If he wants opposition he can have it.' After a moment she returned to stand beside me. She picked up her shoulderbag and stood fingering its strap.

'Aren't you staying to eat with me?'

'No, thanks. I'm going to a late film with friends. They're helping me look for somewhere to share, now Delilah's moved in with Toby.'

'Come round any time you're low and want to talk.'

She nodded. 'Thanks. I will. Oh – I almost forgot: I've heard from Johannes. He's coming over for a holiday next month, fixed himself a package tour. He was angelic to me out there, must have guessed something. He's a nice person, shall you take him on?'

'I'm hoping so.'

'Then shall I bring him round some time?'

'Do that,' I said, and saw her out.

A few days later my breakfast table was enlivened by a Laura-letter:

> Eleanor dearest,
>
> We've seen nothing of you lately. Bill and I are wondering if you'd like a week-end here soon? Do let us know, we'd love to have you.
>
> We think it's curtains between Clare and the boyfriend, thank God. Of course she swans about not speaking when she deigns to come home, but there's something about her *attitude*. We've not heard his name since that Summer School. Of course, we'd like to be *sure* – could you try to get it out of her? We all know you can do *anything*. Bill thinks you maybe had a hand in it? If so, all our love.

Of course, Clare being Clare, she's now just as difficult about something else. Have you heard of some American music place called Tanglewood? Now she's on about that – just think of the cost! It seems that old Strogani's encouraged her, said he'd recommend her for a grant, or something. Would it be a good investment, or should we stand firm? Heaven knows we indulge her enough, and we're getting rather tired of this music racket, just an excuse for fun. Anyway, you can tell us all about it when you come.

And darling, by the way: Clare says that her tiresome Maestro's giving concerts here this autumn, shall you be seeing him? If you do, could you find out if that Toby creature's after a grant too – and if poss. put a spoke in his wheel? I know you'd do anything for little Clare. Not that we've decided to let her go, even if they'll have her.

Do come *soon*, and enjoy a lovely family week-end,

Much love,

Laura

It took willpower not to seize the telephone and tell Laura exactly what I thought of her; only the fear that it might rebound on Clare prevented me. Once I had calmed down I sent a telegram instead:

'Too busy for week-ending. Send Clare Tanglewood at all costs and enjoy well-padded and peaceful old age. Nell.'

22

Clare herself rang me ten days later.

'Nell, are you free tomorrow evening?'

Like a good aunt I said, 'I've a theatre date, but it might be rearranged.'

'Could it? Because Johannes is over here.'

'Then can't you both lunch with me instead? Robin Eustace would love to meet one of my hopefuls.' After Ned's death, Robin had taken over his work at the Agency.

'That would be great, another time. But if you don't mind too much about your theatre we – I'd sooner it was evening. And tomorrow's my one free night.'

'All right, then.' I suppressed a sigh. 'Eight, for supper?'

'Afterwards, I think. Could it be about nine?'

'All right,' I said again, slightly mystified. 'See you then.' As I replaced the receiver I was wondering why she sounded so embarrassed. Well, no doubt I should learn in time. I put it out of my mind.

Next evening she arrived punctually on my doorstep at nine. She was alone. 'What have you done with Johannes, will he find his way all right?' I asked, as we went through into the drawing room.

'He's not coming after all. Or not till later.' She stood fiddling clumsily with a china ornament.

I felt distinctly peeved, after missing a good play.

'Couldn't you have let me know? (Oh, do put that down! It's Chelsea, you'll break it.) Nothing dramatic's happened about you and Toby, has it?' She was wearing black, with a purplish Indian scarf, and might have been in mourning.

'Not about Toby; it's about Johannes. It may be a bit of a shock to you, Nell, it was to me.'

'Oh Clare, I'm so glad,' I said. 'Do come and sit down and tell me about it; he's a charmer too, and I hated seeing you so unhappy.'

She stared at me, then burst out laughing.

'Incurably romantic Nell! What a good thing, really. It's not about me this time, it's about you. I don't know quite how to put this. You won't faint or anything, will you, if I tell you Johannes' father changed his name, after he was in a concentration camp?'

My heart was beating too rapidly, the clock's ticking seemed louder than usual. 'A camp? What's that to do with me? You don't mean . . . it couldn't be – '

'Yes, I do. It is. His name's Franz Walter.'

After a moment I said, 'It can't be, Clare. Franz died in the camp. Johannes is – you must be mistaken.' I don't know why I was so insistent.

'He's not – I'm not. It's Franz Felix Walter. Johannes was coming round with me, but – Nell? You do look peculiar. Shall I call a doctor?'

'Oh Clare, you idiot.'

I stared at her blindly.

Franz dead . . . and now Franz alive. Alive after all these years while I'd been diligently trying to be happy, telling myself there were still things worth living for. But he had married. He hadn't tried to find me, as I'd tried to find him. He had a son.

'Nell,' Clare said at last, 'if you're all right, wouldn't you like to know what happened?'

'Yes . . . yes, of course.'

'It's simple, really. All that confusion, when the war ended. Johannes' father – Franz, I mean – made friends with some people called Spengler when he was in the camp. Georg and Andreas, father and son. They'd had vineyards, over near the

Italian border. They weren't Jews, but they were seized for helping them. The Spengler women – Georg's wife and daughter – weren't taken, they were just warned off, and left to cope as best they could. Old Georg was marvellous, Franz said, so brave. Even in the camp he helped other people. But it was sad, Nell – the son died. He was so beaten up.'

I remembered the violence I had seen done to Franz; nothing, to what could have happened. 'Go on, Clare. Did they – torture Franz too?'

'I think they did.' Clare didn't meet my eyes. 'But he survived, Nell – that's the important thing, isn't it? When his son died the old boy was even more worried about his wife and daughter if *he* didn't survive – he was seventy, and people were dying like flies of starvation and typhoid.'

'They used to drop dead in the streets, even after liberation,' I said. 'It was bad then, even in Vienna.'

'Things got worse in the camp, after the supplies were bombed,' said Clare. 'Ironic, wasn't it? And Georg Spengler knew he couldn't make it – so he made Franz swear to help his family, if he got out alive. He told Franz that though the Nazis would be defeated, there were bad times ahead – some would go free, and they'd probably try to take revenge. Franz had no near relations left, so Spengler told him to say he was his son. He gave Franz a message for his wife and daughter. Something only they would understand, then they'd know he was genuine. Take them my love, he said – if God wills they are alive – and say *I* wish you to take my son's place. They'll need a man to help them.'

I closed my eyes. Oh God. How closely I'd combed the camp records, how easily I could have come face to face with Franz in the centres for displaced people. Destined not to happen, and probably Franz would have preferred it that way.

'So he married the daughter,' I said wearily, 'and she was Johannes' mother. But why did Johannes himself tell you all this? And when?'

'Mostly in Switzerland. Only I didn't put it together with your story, because Johannes didn't tell me his father's real name. After Toby and I split, Johannes and I spent the last evening in a café together. We just sat and talked and talked. About anything. I drank much too much, I know – so did he! God, the things we learned about each other, just about everything, I should think.'

'But, Clare, what's made you realize the connection now?'

'It was Johannes, not me. He went home after the Summer School, and told his father about your offer and Hathaway's.'

'That name would have meant nothing to him.'

'You're wrong, Nell. I'd better tell you the rest. You're sure you're all right?'

I nodded.

'Well, then: the Americans came, and Spengler was dead. Franz got away easily with being his son, because a lot of camp documents had been destroyed in the bombing. Everyone in the camp looked like a skeleton, there was nothing to tell them who he was. They gave him papers, and a pass to go home. A bit awkward, he said, having to find his way! Frau Spengler was shattered by her husband's death, her son's too. She and her daughter almost grabbed at Franz, as a – a mainstay, I suppose.'

'And he was prepared to go on like that, with a false name, indefinitely?' It didn't sound like the proudly independent Franz I'd known; but the horrors of the camps had done strange things to people.

Clare shook her head. 'He stayed a year, helping out. Of course the villagers knew he wasn't Andreas Spengler, but no one gave him away. Then he told Frau Spengler he couldn't live a lie for ever – he wanted to go back to Vienna and tell the authorities.' Clare looked at me sideways. 'The girl was in love with him, I suppose he was pretty attractive, Nell? Anyway, he insisted on going. He got his story confirmed by someone who'd known him in the camps. The Americans were pretty stiff about it at first, he was grilled backwards and forwards and sideways. In the end he was given a clean bill, and new papers.

'Nell – ' another sideways glance – 'it was while he was sitting around in all those offices, trotting from one to the other, that he heard about some woman working for the Red Cross who'd been making inquiries for him months before.'

My hands clasped tight together.

'And was told he was dead.'

'Yes. So he went back to the Americans, and asked them to help him get to England. They made frightful difficulties, and just as he was on the point of giving up, and writing instead, he ran into your friend Gina who was still out there – and she said you'd married Ned Hathaway the week before.'

'Gina? Gina knew this all the time? And never said a word, not even when Ned died.' I jumped up, and walked agitatedly about the room. '*Gina*. I'll never forgive her.'

'But you'd married, Nell. Wouldn't it have been worse to have the world turned upside down again? I bet that's what she thought – I would have. You see, he told her he would go back to the Spengler vineyards, to make a proper job of it. He'd take the old boy's name and carry on the business, which was what Georg Spengler wanted, and support the family. It was something to live for, in that awful post-war world, much as you felt about Ned, I suppose. The two of you didn't have much luck, did you?'

It seemed an understatement. 'But, Clare, I don't understand,' I said slowly. 'Franz rejected me totally . . . or I thought so. What could have changed him, even to think of following me over here?'

'Partly the camps, maybe? The *real* nightmare made the things you'd done, or hadn't, seem unimportant?'

'I should have thought it would make chatting-up the Nazis seem much worse,' I said, rather bitterly.

Clare hesitated. 'I must say, it seemed odd to me, after what you told me. But look, there's more: Johannes says there's something else, something he knows about. He's a bit shy about it, thinks you may mind his knowing! He gave me this for you – ' She opened her bag and drew out a thin package. 'Here, Nell, take it. If you'd like to talk to him tonight we'll ring him, and he'll come over. Or would you rather he came tomorrow, without me?'

I held the package in my hand. It was the size of an ordinary envelope, wrapped in old-fashioned oiled silk.

'Not tonight, Clare. I don't think I could take it. And – forgive me – I'd sooner look at this, whatever it is, alone. Scribble his number for me, and if I feel like it I'll ring him.'

After Clare left I sat for a long while just staring at the package, which was stained with earth or mildew. I opened it at last. Inside it was my letter to Franz, the desperate one I'd sent him at his school, care of his choirmaster. When I spread the pages on my knee something fell out of them – the photograph that Peter or Gina had taken of Franz and me, the day before I left for Bayreuth. It was the ghostliest sensation, to see for the first time that picture of my long-dead self with Franz, smiling happily into camera, our arms around each other and still unaware of looming nightmare.

So my last letter had reached him, after all. But why had he kept it, and the photograph; and how had he kept them through the war years? And if they'd meant something to him why hadn't he replied? Above all, why had he sent them to me now, by the hand of his son?

There seemed to be no answers. I put my hand out to the telephone, but drew back again. I read and re-read that cry of appeal written twenty-eight years ago.

'They were there, hidden in a little cave on the mountain. My father said you would remember it, Mrs. Hathaway. And also how his friend takes the photograph?'

'Yes . . .'

'After *Grossvater* was killed, my father hid in the mountains. He knew all that land so very well. It was then he went for help to his old choirmaster, at Innsbruck. That was when Herr Schmidt gave him your letter.'

'I see . . . not until then.'

But I was thinking less of the letter than of the photograph. Peter must have given it to him some time while Franz still thought the worst of me, and yet he'd kept it as though he cherished it, instead of destroying it as he'd destroyed the letter Tim gave him on the train.

I didn't look at Johannes, although I could sense his fascinated interest. How weird it must all seem to him, and how very long ago. One couldn't really believe in one's own parents' love affairs. Wouldn't that, at least, make it less upsetting for Johannes in relation to his mother? What had Maestro told me about her – that she'd died some years back of TB. Even if he'd loved her, he must have got over any misery by now. It seemed strange to me that Franz had confided in his son.

'I know what you are thinking,' said Johannes. 'It is strange, he confide all this to me?'

'Yes, it is.' I wondered how he saw me. Middle-aged, therefore ancient, fashionably dressed and formidable? Capable, a handler of musical ogres? Probably he and Clare would have a good laugh about it all, specially the cave. And the letter – oh my God, the letter! Even now I felt myself redden as though the old Nell had been resurrected.

'Have you . . . read that letter, Johannes?'

'Yes,' he answered honestly. 'I hope you do not mind too much. I – I could not resist. There is my father, you see, so – always so quiet, so self – ' he wrinkled his nose, floundering for words.

'Self-contained.'

'Much to himself, within himself?'

'Yes, that's it.'

'Well, when I first say your name, Nell – you do not mind if I call you so? – he is very quiet, then he says: you meet the husband too, Johannes? And when I say no, he dies, my father is more quiet; he wills not to talk of you or music further. Then I know something is wrong, and I am quiet too. Three days later, we are walking together in the mountains, and suddenly he is talking about you – and him, as though he cannot help it.'

'Did he tell you what – how it ended?'

Johannes nodded.

'It was blackmail,' I said fiercely. 'They might have killed him in that prison, or beaten him till he was crippled for life. Or they might even have freed him without further harm, how could I tell? How *could* I, Johannes? That was why I – did what I did. But he wouldn't believe that, he tore up my first letter, he said – he said terrible wounding things. Tim, my friend Tim, told me. I made him. Tim had tried so hard to make him listen.' Remembering, I could almost feel again that clawing agony in my chest. 'Now it seems strange to me that when he got my second letter he kept it. And our photograph.'

'It is not strange to me,' said Johannes, with judicial calm. 'What times he lived in, *ja*? He is hurt, furious, then he calms – it is very sweet, your letter, and sad – but already it is too late.'

'After the war he never went back for it. Then he sends you here with it now. For me. Just like that?'

'Yes, and I obey,' said Johannes simply.

We sat in silence.

'Of course, he wants you to have a fine career in music,' I said at last.

'*That* is not why he makes me his courier.'

'No? But if I'm to handle your future we were bound to meet some day. It's less awkward for him, for me, like this. It's a statement, surely. "I kept it – but it's the past. Now look after my son for me."'

'No, Nell, it is not like that. You might never have met him, or known his name. He wants you to know – perhaps he fears too much to come himself. My father is – almost recluse.

He is like that all my life, since the camp. He would not a music career for himself, it is too late, and he commits himself to the land, the vines. The vines are a good life, you shall see how expert my father is. But whenever he must go to the town, on business, he is unhappy till home again. It is a lovely place, by a river. It is truly home. Nell, he asks will you go to see him there? Perhaps stay, when you have time?'

'*No*,' I said violently. 'Oh no, Johannes. It's much too late. Don't worry, it makes no difference to how we handle your career. I'm glad Franz – your father – didn't feel bitter about me, in the end. I'm glad he tried to find me. But we're both different people now, all that was over long ago. It would be stranger meeting stranger. Thank him. Give him my best wishes, always. Tell him, no.'

'But, Nell,' Johannes looked downcast, 'he will be so lonely without me, when I travel.'

('How can I leave my father?' Franz had said.)

'Ridiculous, you old-fashioned child,' I teased him. 'You must have been away at school, surely? And do you think we'd rush passionately into each other's arms, and I'd leave everything here to nurse the vines? What would become of your career, then?'

'You make him and you sound silly, and you are not.'

'No, we're sensible adults, and our lives grew far apart.'

'This mean you will not meet him, ever?' Johannes looked at me like a disappointed child. 'He will be sad, my father. The way he told me – I am sure it means a lot to him.'

I won't be moved by that, I told myself. I will not go to Austria. You cannot resurrect what's dead.

'We shall probably meet one day,' I said lightly. 'Perhaps after some concert, when you're rich and famous. Now I'm rather busy, but you and Clare will dine with me soon, won't you?'

'*Stimmt*, Nell.' But he was looking at me bleakly, disapprovingly, and his jaw had set in a way that reminded me of Franz at his most offended.

'Goodbye, Johannes,' I said firmly. 'Tell Clare to ring me soon.'

Once he had gone I went to my bureau, drew out a folder, and looked long and hard at the contents. My letter to Franz. Our photograph. The crumpled brown petals of a rose that had once been vivid carmine. I had been silly enough to keep it all these years. I put them away and shut the drawer with a slam. '*Liebst du um Schönheit, o mich nicht lieben.*' All over, long ago. As dead and faded as the rose.

23

I heard nothing of Clare nor Johannes for a week, and found myself half-hoping, half-fearing he'd make his career elsewhere. However, they rang the day before my birthday, inviting themselves to dine. I asked Robin Eustace too, he was good at easing situations; and I took trouble with the food and more trouble than usual with my appearance. Johannes looked impressed, and Clare exclaimed, 'Good heavens, Nell! Have I lost an aunt and gained a sister?'

'We'll drink to that,' said Robin, producing his birthday present – some highly superior champagne.

It was a pleasant meal, after all. When we reached the coffee stage Clare murmured, 'We've brought a present for you too, Nell. It was rather expensive, promise you won't waste it?'

'My solemn promise,' I said incautiously and flown with wine. 'What is it – scent?'

Their triumphant expressions should have warned me, as I took the envelope she handed me. Inside was a rail ticket to Innsbruck. I looked up from it not knowing whether to be angry or amused; anyway I was wholly embarrassed. They were bubbling with wicked laughter.

'You did promise us, we have a witness,' said Johannes solemnly.

'Your secretary told me you were taking a long week-end off, to redecorate your flat; I wormed it out of her,' said Clare. 'So no backing out, Nell! I'll supervise the decorators while you're – er, visiting past scenes. Sorry we couldn't possibly afford the air-fare. Still, this way's more like the first time, isn't it?'

I looked at them speechlessly, and they grew hysterical.

'What's this secret joke?' asked Robin.

'It's no joke at all, it's a form of blackmail!'

'I am sure, when I tell him of your promise, that my father meets you himself,' said Johannes. 'With a little bouquet, perhaps?' he added kindly. (Franz must have been very explicit.) 'And since it is so important to us all, Clare and I will put you on the train.'

'Ah, I understand,' said Robin. 'Agency business. Don't worry, Johannes, you've not seen Nell in action. Your father may mean to resist, but he hasn't a hope.' And couldn't understand why I glared at him, and Johannes and Clare laughed so much that Clare fell off her chair.

'Truly,' I said, 'you've forced me into an embarrassing mistake. How would you have liked me to boss you and Toby so?'

Clare turned away her face. I touched her arm, murmured, 'I'm sorry,' contritely, and suffered myself to be led down the platform to the waiting train – no steam engine but a diesel, powerful and prosaic. The romance of steam was over, too. These absurd creatures beside me were mad to think the past could be brought to life again. At least Franz and I could meet on common ground regarding Johannes' career.

'Come on, Nell, in you get. Here's your nice corner seat.'

They stood behind me and almost pushed me into the carriage. Johannes slung my case on to the rack.

I said helplessly, 'Clare, Johannes, it's not so simple as you think it is.'

'We both think all these difficulties you're making are a good sign! If you didn't care at all you'd whizz off like a bird, and spend your time there arguing over percentages for Johannes.'

'Do that anyway, Nell. Large percentages.' Johannes took

my hand and kissed it. He looked very like his father, and I could have hit him.

'You horrid bullying pair,' I murmured, kissing Clare goodbye. They left me with magazines and papers, and stood waving as the slow departing glide began. Their dwindling figures recalled memories of my father, immaculately dressed in city suit and bowler, seeing me off from this same platform all those years ago.

Time past, time present. No misty trails of smoke. Shadow and sun on the rail banks . . . yet it was later in the year, the light more golden and mature, a hint of deadness in the leaves, a chill breeze blowing. The wheels seemed to run, the train to sway to the ominous rhythm of 'mistake, mistake, mistake'.

It was a long while since I'd been abroad except by air. In Paris there was time for coffee at the station. As darkness fell an eerie sense of ghosts travelling with me grew stronger: shutting my eyes I should surely hear Cassie's grumbling, Gina's laughter; sense Tim's presence in the next carriage, or suffer Tommy's reprimands for unladylike conduct – but she was dead too, five years ago. I shivered. It was sad, it was madness, to be taking this gruesome journey. How could I have been so weak as to keep the promise tricked out of me by Clare and Johannes? People were always tricking me into promises that it was wrong to keep. Look at Korbinion.

That settled it. I would leave the train at Zurich and fly home. I would wire Franz. Probably he was having second thoughts already.

I turned *my* thoughts deliberately to planning the strategy for Johannes' future. Franz too might find that a pleasant form of co-operation, by letter of course. And I must force Bill and Laura into getting extra tuition for Clare, and introduce her myself to that new young Management, and see that she really worked before she went to Tanglewood.

Pleased with myself for being so strongminded, I shut my eyes and drifted into sleep.

A sudden jerk woke me. It must be hours later, for the train was standing at a station. Zurich! I scrambled to my feet, pushing heavy locks of hair out of my eyes. Lord, I must look a sight. They were dear children, but they hadn't thought I might like a couchette, or perhaps it was too expensive. I dragged my case from the rack, and clambered over protesting forms, terrified the train might start before I could escape. In my haste I almost fell on to the platform, dropping the case and stumbling over it.

An arm went round me and supported me. Franz's laughing voice said, 'All these long, long years, and you are still falling on to platforms with your holdall, *lieb'* Nell?'

'You – you were meeting me at Innsbruck,' I stammered.

'Which is why you make the so-logical escape at Zurich, yes? This I expect, and the little Clare rings yesterday and says, "Quick, quick to Zurich and meet her with your car, we do not trust her". So I wait long, afraid you have escape at Paris. Oh, Nell! And Johannes says to bring the little bouquet, he wish to travel freely in future, and not worry that he leaves Papa behind.'

'Franz.'

The flowers were the mirror image of the ones he had given me twenty-seven – eight – years ago. I looked into his face, and the twenty-eight years were visible, made crueller by the harsh night lighting. The years and the suffering. Johannes hadn't warned me about the gauntness, and the scar that ran oblique and jagged from his forehead to his chin. But it was still the face I had so dearly loved.

'Nell, why do you cry? Did you not forgive me long ago?'

'There was never anything for me to forgive.'

'Wasn't there? That is so generous. And what you did was heroic, later I knew. And I knew too – remember? *"Dich lieb' ich, immer, immerdar".'*

I couldn't speak. I just stood clutching the flowers.

'That rose does not need watering! *"Liebst du um liebe, o ja mich liebe." Ja,* Nell? Life is so short, now. Please, *ja*?'